HARRIET
OF
HARE STREET

Angela Rigley

Angela Rigley

ISBN: 978-1717376664
      1717376665
Copyright belongs to the author

British Library Cataloguing in Publication data.

Published by Angela Rigley
www.nunkynoo.yolasite.com

I dedicate this book to the memory of my late mother, Freda Alice Briggs, neé Knight, who was a true cockney, born in the East End of London. She lost her older brother, who had enlisted in the army, to tuberculosis, her father when she was thirteen, and her mother at eighteen. Although not a biography, many of the events in this book mirror circumstances in her life.

The word *cockalorum* is used in the sense of a 'loved one' as my mother used to call me, although modern dictionaries cite it as meaning a self-important person.

Other books by the author:
Looking for Jamie
A Dilemma for Jamie
School for Jamie
Choices for Jamie
Rewards for Jamie
Florence and the Highwayman
Nancie
Lea Croft
The Peacock Bottle
My Book of Silly Poems and Things

Cal the Caveboy
Cal Saves his Sister
Cal's Good Idea
Baarlie the Naughty Lamb
Baarlie and the Snow
Baarlie Wants to Fly
Dotty and Raggy are Lost in the Woods
Dotty is Lost
My Silly Poems for Kids

Chapter 1

December 1894

Dark clouds loomed overhead and a hush fell over the busy street as Harriet Harding hurried from the shop. Spots of rain fell on her tatty bonnet and a shiver ran down her back. Was it an omen of doom?

She drew her shawl around her slender shoulders. Her thin coat didn't offer much protection, but she didn't own a pelisse. Would she make it home before the heavens opened? The sun had been shining when she'd picked up the shopping list on her way home from school on that crisp December day. Maybe she should have gone across to Old Mother Peele and asked her opinion. The old sage always knew about the weather.

The instant she reached the front door to number four Hare Street it opened. Her mother grabbed the bag of groceries and urged her inside the lounge. "My dearie, you'll catch your death of cold. Come inside, girl, come in. Why didn't you borrow my warm coat?"

"I didn't know it was going to rain, Mama." She didn't mention the premonition. Her mother didn't believe in such things.

Taking a quick look in the mirror above the empty fireplace, she pushed her long, brown, curly hair off her forehead. It always became curlier when damp. Why couldn't she have been blessed with straight hair like her mother's? Apparently, curly hair suited her, and she wouldn't like it straight. But she would have welcomed the chance to find out.

"Your father should be home any time," called her mother over her shoulder as she put the food in the pantry. "I hope he remembered his umbrella."

"He did, Mama. I wondered why he took it on such a fine day."

"Your father is very practical, that's why. You'd do well to copy him, instead of living in your own little cocoon, flitting about like a will-o-the-wisp."

"Mama, I do not." Miffed, she dropped a small pack of butter onto a dish. "You didn't tell me to buy this, but Papa loves it. He deserves a treat." Not you, though, after chiding me like that.

"How thoughtful of you. Did you have any trouble asking for tick?"

Regretting her evil thoughts, Harriet shook her head.

Her mother continued, "I hope the bread isn't chalky today. I suppose Missus Green saves the chalky loaves for us because we only pay her on Fridays when your father collects his wages."

"She was very pleasant today. Mind you, that new lady who's just moved in up our side of the street was in the shop. I suppose she wanted to impress her."

Missus Harding patted her swollen belly. "I'll bet Missus Green doesn't sell her chalky loaves. Well, she needn't come all high and mighty, just because she used to live in a big house with servants, and owned a carriage. My grandfather was well-off. If it hadn't been for my uncle squandering all his money, we wouldn't be living here."

Harriet had heard the story many times, but she allowed her mother to rant. Then she asked, "Speaking of grandfathers, when's Gampy coming home from sea?"

"Child, why do you still call him by that babyish name? Can't you say, 'Grandfather', like any normal thirteen-year old?"

With a sigh, she replied, "Because he likes me calling him Gampy. He says thinking about me keeps him sane while he's at sea all those months. I can't wait to hear more of his adventures."

Her mother pinned a stray lock of greying hair into place and sat down. "He makes up most of them."

"You always say that, but I believe them, especially the one about the pirates. That must have been exciting. Fancy, actual pirates climbing aboard his ship! And the tale about the black cat appearing from nowhere in the middle of a storm. They all thought it was the devil."

A tut and a shake of the head was her reply.

"Anyway, Mama, you didn't answer me. When will he be home?" Harriet filled the kettle, put it on the range, and chose two cups and saucers with the fewest chips.

"Before long, I should think. He's been away six months now. He doesn't even know about this here baby." She patted her stomach again.

"I've been wondering, Mama, how did it get inside you?"

"What?"

"The baby?"

"Oh, um…I'll tell you another day. We need to start your father's dinner. You know he likes it on the table when he walks in from his job at the docks."

"But…"

"No more questions. Peel those potatoes."

Last time she had asked the question her mother had told her the fairies would be visiting her shortly, as they did all girls of her age. She hadn't seen any yet. She had been speculating for days, even feeling her own belly, to see if had grown, in case she might have a baby inside. But it remained as flat as ever.

Her grandfather might tell her. She'd ask him when he returned. They would be more cramped, but she didn't mind. Her older brother, William Henry—named after him, with the Henry added—had joined the militia. He would be away for a long time in Hampshire, half a day's journey from London.

A loud knock on the door made them both jump.

"Who can be banging like that?" cried her mother as Harriet hurried to open it.

A man in red military uniform stood on the doorstep. For a second, Harriet thought her musings had conjured up her brother, but the man was older, and severe-looking. "Mistress Harding?" he asked in a gruff voice.

Her mother came up behind her. "Yes, that's me."

The man took off his hat. "Captain Holmes, ma'am. Please may I come in?"

"Yes, yes, of course, how discourteous. Pray, excuse my daughter's bad manners."

Harriet puffed out her cheeks, about to protest but, seeing her mother's worried face, thought better of it. "Would you like a cup of tea?" she asked.

The gentleman shook his head. "No, thank you. I regret I am the bearer of bad news."

"Bad news?" her mother asked in a weak voice.

"Pray, sit down, Mistress Harding."

Harriet took her mother's proffered hand and gripped it, wondering what bad news he was about to impart. Surely nothing to do with her brother? He was, as she had been remembering, in Aldershot.

The man asked, "Is your husband due home?" At her mother's nod, he continued, "Perhaps we should wait until he comes." He gave a pointed look at her belly. "It would be better if he were with you."

From the straight-backed armchair, her mother looked up with such a sad face that Harriet put her arms around her, fearing the worst. They waited, listening to the ticking of the old grandfather clock on the wall and their uneven breathing, for what seemed like hours, but was probably only ten to fifteen minutes.

The man shifted his position and took a deep breath. At one point he seemed about to speak, but remained silent, prolonging the uneasy atmosphere.

Should she offer to finish cooking the dinner? They had only peeled the vegetables, not put them to boil. And the sausages... What would her father say when he came in?

"Mama, shall I...?" she began but before she could finish, the front door opened and her father backed in, shaking out his umbrella before shutting the door.

"What's that carriage outside?" he began. He turned and saw their visitor. "Oh, I beg your pardon..."

The military man stepped forward and bowed. "Good day, Mister Harding. Captain Holmes at your service."

Her father looked around with wide eyes, replying. "Good day, sir. I trust I find you well."

"Yes, sir, very well, thank you, but..."

"Pray, let me pour you a drink." Her father approached the cabinet where he kept a bottle of brandy but, with a shake of the head, the man refused. "A cup of tea, then? Freda, what are you about, not offering the gentleman refreshment?"

"Mister Harding, pray, sit down." The man urged her father onto the couch.

His drawn face not at all his usual ruddy complexion, her father's eyes darted around the room as he wrung his hands. "It's William, isn't it?" he asked in a tight voice.

"Yes, sir, he's had an accident. He is very poorly."

Her father let out a loud breath. "Thank God. I thought you were going to say he was dead."

"Well, sir, he might not survive the night."

Her mother gasped as she let go of Harriet's hands and sat forward, asking. "Wh...what happened?"

The captain shifted awkwardly. "I regret I am not at liberty to say."

Her mother covered her face with her hands. "Thomas, we must go to him." She turned to the man. "Would you be able to take us? We don't have transport."

"Well, ma'am, in your condition..."

"Damn my condition. I need to see my son."

Expecting her father to exclaim at the language, Harriet drew in her breath, but he stood up and walked around the little room, nodding in agreement. "Yes, please, sir, as my wife says, is that possible?"

"May I come, too?" she asked.

"No, child," answered her mother. "A military camp is not the place for a young girl."

"But, Mama…"

"Don't start one of your tantrums, Harriet," replied her father. "Your mother said no."

What did he mean? She never argued and, surely she had a right to see her brother? But once her father had made up his mind… She stalked into the kitchen and took a bite of a carrot and crunched. Unable to hear what they were saying, she returned, asking, "What about dinner, Papa? Should I make it for your return?"

"No, child," replied her mother. "We'll be away for a day or two."

"But what about me?"

Her father glared at her with such an angry face she recoiled. "Everything doesn't revolve around you," he stated.

Her mother tried to pacify her. "Your father isn't himself, dearie. Don't be upset by his manner." She scowled at him and he turned away. "We'll arrange for you to stay with a neighbour. What about your friend, Lucy? I'm sure her mother wouldn't object."

"Lucy will be at work in the shop."

"Well, pop round and check while we make our arrangements."

Harriet looked at the clock. Would her friend be home yet? Not wanting to incur more of her father's wrath, she grabbed a coat from behind the door.

Chapter 2

It had stopped raining, and the sun shone. That cheered her as she made her way to her friend's house. A knock on the door produced no reply. She could have opened it and called, in case the occupants were in the back yard, but she carried on, past the street vendors, selling meat pies and jellied eels, to the end of the run-down street in Bethnal Green in the East End of London. There she stood under the viaduct, to escape the smells and noises of Hare Street. She'd grown up with the stench from the neighbours' back yards, especially those who kept pigs. Her mother ensured the night soil men collected their waste, and looked down on neighbours on the other side of the street, even Old Mother Peele, although now and again she might lower her standards to ask for her advice.

A train rumbled above her, puffing out thick, black smoke. How she yearned to take a ride on one. Her father kept promising to treat her, but she was still waiting.

What would it mean to her if her brother died? She missed his practical jokes, like the time he'd hidden her one and only necklace, pretending he'd taken it to the pawnbroker. She'd whacked him that hard when he confessed, he'd had a black eye for days. He'd saved her from a scolding from their father by pretending he'd walked into a door. How thoughtful he could be when he wasn't teasing her.

She ought to return home. Skirting past the pitiful beggar children on the side of the road, she called at Lucy's house once more.

Missus Bowe opened the door. "Yes, of course you may stay, my dear," she replied, when Harriet told her the situation. "When are your parents going?"

"Immediately, I think."

"Should your mother be haring across the country in her condition? She doesn't want to put the baby at risk."

Harriet shrugged. If her mother was determined, nothing would stop her, especially when it concerned her 'pride and joy'—her only son.

The carriage stood outside her house, the horse snorting and stamping its hooves, with the driver trying to stop the ragged children from tormenting it. He nodded to her. Should she acknowledge him? Her mother often warned her not to speak to strangers, but as this man would be carting her parents off, she nodded back.

Her mother's bonnet tied, and her grey shawl covering her best green dress, she asked, "Where have you been, child? We've been waiting. What did Missus Bowe say? Can she have you?"

She didn't know which question to answer first. "Yes, Mamma, she said I may stay with them. Do you have any idea how long you'll be away?"

"As long as it takes," replied her father before her mother had chance to open her mouth. "It depends how poorly your brother is."

"Is he going to die?"

Her mother gave her a cuddle. With tears in her eyes she replied, "We must all be brave, and pray to God that it be His will to save William. Will you do that, dearie?"

"Yes, Mama. I'll pray extra hard." She turned to her father and after a moment's hesitation he took her in his arms and hugged her.

"You still mind your manners, mind. Just because we are not here, doesn't mean you can let them drop."

"Yes, Papa."

After more kisses and hugs, her father picked up the tapestry bag and they said their farewells. Harriet waved until they had rounded the corner, and closed the door, shutting out the traffic. Did she dare stay on her own? They would never know. But the bogey-man might find her, or the headless horseman Lucy's brother had told her about. His big black horse had piercing eyes and a foaming mouth, and he had no head, obviously, since he was called the headless horseman. But how would he know she'd be on her own, or enter the house if she locked the door? Better not take the chance.

She put the vegetables in a saucepan of water, and the sausages into the meat safe in the pantry. Hopefully, her parents would be home the following day, and she could welcome them with a tasty meal.

Lucy's father had been off work due to a back injury caused by an accident on the railway. Unsure if he had gone back, Harriet sat down to wait, in case Lucy had not yet returned, and picked up an old, earmarked copy of Girl's Own. A neighbour had given her the comic and she loved the stories and poems.

After reading the stories for the hundredth time, Harriet set the paper down, wondering what else to do. Her mother's darning mushroom, with one of her father's socks, stared at her from the side table. Finish that? No, her handiwork wasn't good enough, according to her mother. What else? The baby jacket started with blue wool unpicked from one of her old jumpers? But without her mama to pick up any stitches she dropped, it would end up ruined. Most girls knew how to knit, but she was useless, no matter how many times her mother showed her how to do it.

Where was the book she'd started the previous week about a boy who asked for more gruel, called Oliver something or other? Lucy's older brother had lent it to her before going off to work on a farm, miles away.

As she felt down the back of the couch a knock startled her. Who was calling at that late hour? All their friends opened the door and popped their heads round without waiting for an answer. Tiptoeing over to take a peek through a chink in the green curtain, she hoped it wasn't a stranger.

A woman in a tatty black coat, full of holes, stood with her back to the window. When she turned, Harriet spotted a baby in her arms. What did she want? Curiosity overtook any fears. She lifted the latch and opened the door a crack. "Yes?" she asked in a squeaky voice?

"Is Bill 'ome?"

She narrowed the gap. "Nobody called Bill lives here."

The woman began to cry. Harriet opened the door wider. The visitor was only about her age. Over her shoulder, she noticed neighbours peering through their curtains. "Please don't cry," she pleaded but, without saying another word, the woman shoved the baby into her arms and ran off.

"Hey!" she shouted, running after her. "Hey, come back. I don't want a baby." The woman turned the corner, her sobs loud, as Harriet tried to catch up, but she was hampered by the unusual bundle and lost sight of her in the crowd.

What should she do? She had no idea how to look after a baby. Her mother had borne a boy two years before, and she had watched her feed him, but he died. Go for advice to Missus Bowe, or maybe Old Mother Peele? Yes, ask the wise old sage.

She crossed the road and knocked on her door. Nobody went into that woman's house uninvited. Heaving the infant into a more comfortable position, she waited for a reply.

It soon came. "What's this then?"

"It's a baby."

"I can see that. Who was that woman what left it?"

"I don't know, ma'am. She asked for someone called Bill and plonked the baby in my arms."

"You'd better come in." The door opened wide and Old Mother Peele gestured for her to enter the untidy room, filled with shelves of knick-knacks and potions.

She held out the baby but the old woman shuddered, as if afraid of it. "Put it on the couch." She puffed out her cheeks and made a peculiar sound with her lips.

Harriet did as bid, and unwrapped the shawl. A letter fell onto the floor. She picked it up.

"Let me see." Old Mother Peele grabbed it from her. "Oh, dear, oh, dearie me," she muttered as she read it.

"What? What does it say?"

"Either your father has been a naughty boy, or its mother mistook the address."

"What do you mean?"

Several neighbours sneaked in.

"Show me." One of them took the letter. "What are you going to do?"

"Me?" asked Harriet. "I haven't the faintest idea. Let me read it."

The letter, written by an uneducated person read, 'carnt coap babie is yours.'

"Oh, 'eck," exclaimed one of the other women. "See if there's anything else."

Harriet took off the baby's shawl, revealing a dirty, cotton nightdress and a wet nappy.

The baby smiled. "Ah, it likes you," muttered the first neighbour.

"What sex is it? Doesn't look like a girl," said one of the others, pulling down the front of the nappy. "Ah, a boy. I thought as much."

"How old do you think he is?"

"Six or seven months, I should say."

"Shall I find a constable?" asked another woman.

"The police wouldn't be interested in an abandoned baby."

Harriet wanted to sneak out and leave them to it, but Old Mother Peele caught her eye. "You'll need to make a decision, girl. Where's your mother gone?" she asked.

"She and Papa have gone to Aldershot to see my brother," Harriet explained, adding, "At least we have baby clothes and things at home, with Mama expecting. I'll change him, but I can't feed him."

The women all laughed, looking at her flat chest. Little buds were growing, but they would be no use.

"I'll do that," suggested a neighbour who had not long arrived. "My John's almost weaned. He won't mind sharing." She picked up the grizzling baby and cooed to it. "He's hungry. I'll take him now, and I have a dress John's grown out of."

"Thank you, thank you." Relief flooded through Harriet as the crowd filed out of the small room and stood on the pavement, muttering and discussing her situation. She was desperate for a drink and her stomach rumbled. What to do for the best? Go straight to Missus Bowe's house or go home? Unused to making decisions, she dithered.

Chapter 3

Thirst overtook Harriet's uncertainty and she popped home for a glass of water. The mere idea of her with a baby was ludicrous. How would she manage? Perhaps the lady who had taken him to feed might like another? At least she lived on the right side of the street. But two babies at once? One of her neighbours had twins, and she coped. Why shouldn't Missus…? What was her name? Wood? Or Forest? Twig? Branch? Leaf? *Now you're being stupid.* A bubble of hysteria brewed in her throat and she sat at the table. What the heck were her parents going to say when they returned? Well, they shouldn't have left her. Then she wouldn't be in such a pickle. The women had seemed to think he was her father's baby, but he couldn't be; her papa was married to her mother and was a wonderful husband, trusted by everyone.

On the way out, her stomach rumbled, and she took a carrot and chomped on it.

Three boys were playing football, and the ball rolled towards her. She kicked it, hitting the window of a house opposite. With a collective "Oo" the boys turned to her in horror. When they saw the window wasn't broken, they scooped up the ball and ran up the street. With a sigh, Harriet thanked her guardian angel that nobody had come chasing after her. She didn't want another blot on her copy book.

A girl of five or six, with curly ginger hair, came up to her. "Are you the lady what owns that baby me ma's feeding?"

"If you mean the…" What was the word she needed? Her own father had been one. He'd been found in a basket in a church doorway. A foundling—that was it. "If you mean the foundling, then it isn't mine, I just happened to…to… Anyway, I was hoping your ma might keep it."

"No, she says she can't. She says we can't afford another mouth to feed." The girl twiddled with her apron. "She says when are you coming to fetch it?"

Her heart dropped. "Has she finished feeding it?"

"She says…"

"Your ma says a lot of things, doesn't she?"

The girl nodded.

Harriet had seen the child before but, as her mother did not allow her to socialise much, she had never spoken to her. "What's your name?" she asked, to jog her memory.

"Isabel."

"Ah, how pretty."

"Tell me yours."

"It's Harriet. Harriet Alice Loxley Harding."

"Ooer, that's funny. I ain't got a middle one. Me ma says me pa don't agree with having more than one."

Harriet laughed. "Well, I'm proud of my names. My grandfather's mother was a Loxley, and my mama says we should remember our heritage."

Isabel pulled a face. "Them's big words."

"Are all your brothers and sisters ginger?"

"No, only me. Me ma says I'm special. That's her, up there."

A woman approached, carrying two babies. She held out the new arrival to Harriet. "He's all fed and changed."

Harriet kept her arms behind her back. "Couldn't you keep him a little while longer, Missus…?"

"Missus Leekes."

"Ah." Nothing to do with trees at all, just vegetables.

"No, I can't. Much as I'd like to help out, I don't have the room. I can feed him every now and again, but that's all."

"But I don't know what to do with a baby. Our Tommy died. What if it was my fault? This one might die too." Tears welled up in her eyes as she considered being responsible for the child's death.

18

Missus Leekes handed her own baby to Isabel and eased the new one into Harriet's arms. "You can't have been to blame for your brother's death. He was sickly. This one seems healthy, although thin. Come on, let's take him inside."

"I'm supposed to be staying with Missus Bowe. I'll ask her if I can take him there."

"Yes, yes, you do that." Missus Leekes took her own baby from her daughter, who almost dropped him as he wriggled in her little arms. "I'll feed him again in the morning, so don't you worry about that."

"But...but..." Harriet swallowed hard. He had fallen asleep, but he might not sleep for long.

"Good girl." Missus Leekes patted her shoulder. "Come on, Issy, your father's waiting for his dinner." She left, leaving Harriet staring at the bundle in her arms. What should she do? Go home, or ask Missus Bowe if she could take him there? Decisions, decisions.

As she debated, the lady in question came out. "Ah, it's true. They said you'd been lumbered with a baby. I didn't know whether to believe them."

"Yes, Missus Bowe, and I haven't the faintest idea what to do." Screwing up her face, she looked up at the lady.

"Here, give him to me. It's a boy, isn't it?" At Harriet's nod, she continued, "We'll all muck in and look after him."

Harriet wanted to cry with relief. "Ah, Missus Bowe, thank you. I've been praying you'd say that. God must have been listening for a change. I'll find some clothes." She ran into the house and rummaged in a drawer, pulling out a dress. "Will this fit him?"

Missus Bowe laughed. "No, that'd fit a new-born. This little man looks about six or seven months old."

"I'll check upstairs, then. Ma saved little Tommy's things for the new baby. I won't be a mo." She had never entered her parents' bedroom without being invited. But needs must, as her mother often said. The door creaked as she opened it. Now, which drawer?

"Have you found anything?" called up Missus Bowe.

"No, not yet."

"Never mind. He'll do for tonight. We'll take another look in the morning."

Good idea, thought Harriet, reluctant to poke around in her mother's belongings.

A noise came from the corner of the ceiling nearest the window. Startled, she looked up. Only a few cobwebs, one with a fly in it. "Serves you right," she muttered. "You shouldn't have been there in the first place."

"Who were you talking to?" asked Missus Bowe when she returned downstairs.

"Um, was I?"

"I thought I heard you."

"Just a fly."

"As long as you weren't trying to attract my attention. Come along, let's put this little one to bed."

Harriet closed the door behind her and glanced up at the roof. A blackbird sat on the gutter. That must have been the noise.

"I wonder what his name is," she said when they entered the Bowes' small living room.

"Didn't the note say?"

She took the paper out of her apron pocket and reread it. "Nope. I can't see anything like a name. Here." She held it out.

"Let me lay him down first." Missus Bowe carried the baby upstairs.

Harriet looked around. She had been inside the house before, playing with Lucy and their dolls, but had never noticed the pictures on the walls, or the toby jugs in the cabinet in the corner.

"How about Archibald?" suggested Missus Bowe as she came back down.

Harriet shook her head. "No, I don't like that. I have an uncle with that name. He smacked me for being rude."

"Well, if you were rude, then you deserved it." The lady cleared her embroidery from an armchair. "Sit yourself down, girlie, and I'll check the dinner. Mister Bowe should be home any minute, and Lucy."

"Are you sure you have enough? Do you want me to fetch the carrots Mama and me prepared?"

"No need for that. There'll be plenty. Ah, here he is now."

Chapter 4

The door opened and in walked Lucy. "Phew, what a day…" she began, and noticed Harriet. "Oo, hello."

"Harriet's here because her brother's poorly and her parents have gone to see him," explained Missus Bowe, before Harriet could say anything,

"That's good. I mean, not that your brother…" Lucy's voice tailed off as the door opened again and her father came in. "Good evening, Papa." She kissed him as he hobbled inside. "Let me take your coat."

As he allowed her to help him, he scowled at Harriet from under his bushy eyebrows. She shrunk against the back of the couch. What if he didn't agree to her staying? His wife explained again why she was. His scowl remained, although he didn't speak, merely went through to the kitchen, and she could hear him washing his hands.

First lap over. She knew the phrase as her father enjoyed a flutter on the racehorses, when he had a spare penny or two, and would sometimes discuss their form and the races with her. How many laps there would be with Mister Bowe, she didn't know. Hopefully, not too many.

His wife called her into the kitchen and she sat in the place indicated. Lucy reached over and patted her hand. She hadn't seemed as welcoming as Harriet had thought she would be. Maybe she was tired after a busy day at work.

They tucked in to the meal of roly-poly pudding and potatoes.

"This is delicious, Missus Bowe," offered Harriet. "I wish my ma made dishes like this."

Another scowl from Mister Bowe stopped her and she ate the food in dainty little portions. Her father had told her off once for shovelling food into her mouth. She didn't want this man to do the same.

They finished the meal in silence, the only sounds being the scraping of cutlery on the plates, and a grunting noise Mister Bowe made as he chewed. Harriet tried not to look at him, in case she giggled. He reminded her of the pigs her neighbours kept in their back yards. She caught the eye of his wife, and looked down, hoping the lady hadn't realised what she'd been thinking.

Missus Bowe cleared the empty dishes. "I'm sorry there's no afters, today. What with everything that's happened, I haven't had time to make one."

Her husband sat back and wiped his mouth with the back of his hand. "That's a pity, my dear. I'd been looking forward to your rice pudding."

"I like the skin. Do you, Harriet?" asked Lucy as they stood up.

"I…" She glanced across at the father, wondering it was all right for her to speak. He watched her with his eyebrows raised, as if expecting a reply. "I don't know. My pa always has it," she answered.

Mister Bowe sighed, as if disappointed in her reply.

"Ah, I nearly forgot, dear husband…" began his wife, but looking at Harriet pointedly.

I suppose she's going to tell him about the baby, she thought. *I was wondering when she'd bring it up. I daren't.*

His face softened as he listened to the story, not at all the reaction she had been expecting, and Lucy clapped her hands in glee. "Oo, a baby, how wonderful."

"Well, I wouldn't put it like that," replied her mother.

"May I see him?"

"As long as you're quiet and don't wake him. I'll wash up while you're gone."

"I'll help when I come down."

"No, it's all right. Keep very quiet, mind."

Lucy grabbed Harriet's hand and dragged her up the stairs. The baby lay on the floor surrounded by cushions, making little sucking movements with his mouth. She

23

stroked his face, whispering, "Isn't he cute? What's his name?"

Harriet shook her head. "We don't know," she mouthed, backing out of the room. She didn't want him waking, for she might have to do something with him. "I'd like to call him Tommy," she declared, once they were downstairs. "After my little brother who died."

Missus Bowe nodded as she lit another candle. "Yes, that's a good idea." She sat down and picked up her darning mushroom to mend a hole in a grey cardigan. "Tommy it is."

Harriet smiled at Lucy who smiled back and picked up a pack of cards. "Shall we play a game Old Maid?"

Mister Bowe lit his pipe, and the smoke drifted towards them. Not with the sweet smell of her father's tobacco. It almost choked her as she opened her mouth to reply, and she turned away and covered her face as she nodded.

"Pa, do you have to smoke that smelly stuff?" asked Lucy as she dealt the cards.

He lay back, his legs stretched out in front of him, one of them on a stool, clearly the one he had injured. "You know what you can do if you don't like it."

"It might upset the baby upstairs."

"Ha, it never upset you, so I'm not stopping now for some waif we don't know." With the end of his penknife, he poked the tobacco in the pipe and puffed even more, blowing out the smoke between his teeth, his lips curled back.

Lucy shrugged, whispering, "I'm sorry about that."

Harriet shook her head. It wasn't her friend's fault. And why shouldn't the man do as he pleased in his own house?

"How did work go, today?" his wife asked him.

Harriet concentrated on the game, not listening to the conversation between the two older people. "Do you have Mister Baker?" she asked Lucy.

They finished the game and began another. A sound came from above. Harriet froze. Had the baby woken up? She glanced across at Missus Bowe. Had she heard it? Apparently not, for she was still darning. Should she go up and see? No, best leave it. She strained her ears to listen for the sound again, but nothing came. Phew.

"Aren't you going for your usual?" Missus Bowe asked her husband.

He tapped out the pipe into the hearth. "Yes, I may as well. Too much female company can be..."

"Well, you shouldn't have driven our Bernard away, then you'd have male company."

"Don't start, woman." He took his coat off the hook on the back of the door and went out.

Lucy's younger brother had run away to sea some years before, but Harriet didn't know the circumstances. Maybe someone would enlighten her, but neither Lucy nor her mother seemed as if they wanted to. She yawned, setting off a chain of reaction, as both Lucy and her mother did also.

"If nobody minds, I think I'll go to bed," said Lucy, putting the cards back in their box. "Ma, where's Harriet sleeping?"

Missus Bowe put down her work and stretched. "Would you mind sleeping on the floor next to the baby...I mean Tommy? I could find you a blanket and a pillow."

"That wouldn't be very comfortable," replied Lucy. "Sleep in my bed with me. There's plenty of room. I don't snore."

Harriet laughed. She had not fancied sharing with the baby. What if she woke him by turning over, or lying on top of him? "Thank you, if you're sure you don't mind."

Lucy yawned again. "You might be disturbed when I get up in the morning to go to work."

"That won't matter. I'm usually an early bird. I like to be up and about."

"Good, that's settled then. I'll just nip out to the privy."

Chapter 5

The baby slept through the night without waking and Missus Leekes fed him again, and changed him into clean clothes. She also brought round an old baby carriage she had borrowed from a neighbour.

Harriet took him for a walk, not knowing what else to do. As the day had started out sunny, but remembering the previous day when she had been caught in the sudden downpour, she grabbed an extra blanket. Her shawl around her shoulders, she pushed the carriage towards the park at the end of the street, her little haven away from the squalor of the neighbourhood. She sat on a bench, listening to the birds. Landaus and other carriages drove past, with ladies in fancy clothes, holding their parasols to protect their faces from the wintry sun. She deliberately held her face up to it, to feel its warm rays on her cheeks.

Would she be in trouble for missing school? She only had a few weeks left, and would then have to look for a job. What could she do that would satisfy her father? He said he didn't want his daughter to work in one of the many factories, but maybe she could go into service. She liked the thought of wearing one of those maids' uniforms.

A lady she assumed to be a nanny, from her black clothes, approached with a little girl dressed in a red coat and bonnet, and sat next to her. She peered into the perambulator. "Is this your baby brother or sister?"

"Well, sort of."

"Either he or is or isn't."

The nanny let the little girl run off, with a warning not to go far. Harriet couldn't be bothered to explain the situation with the baby again. "His name's Tommy."

"I have a brother called Tommy. Is his real name Thomas?"

What a lot of questions. The lady didn't look much older than herself.

"Yes," she agreed, because it was simpler.

The little girl fell over, and the nanny jumped up to rescue her. She slapped her legs and shouted, "I told you to be careful. Now look what you've done. Your coat is filthy dirty. What will your mama say when we return home?" She slapped the child again and shook her, making her scream all the more. Harriet wanted to interfere, but thought better of it. The nanny's face told her she might start on her if she did.

"Just look at that," retorted the nanny when she sat down again. "I'll be blamed, you know. Her mother will say it's all my fault for not taking proper care of her, but how can I make her sit still for hours on end? I thought bringing her for a walk would tire her out and she'd sleep when we returned."

The little girl put her thumb in her mouth and leant her head on the nanny's chest.

"She looks like she'll sleep now," suggested Harriet, rocking the perambulator, in case the girl's screams had disturbed her own charge.

"That'll do no good. I can't carry her all the way home," grumbled the nanny.

Some people are never satisfied, thought Harriet. *She wanted the little girl to go to sleep and now she has, she's moaning.*

With a deep sigh, the nanny stood up, carrying the child over her shoulder. "I shall have to. It's just as well we don't have far to go."

Harriet watched her trudge across the park, nudging the child upwards each time she slipped down. Maybe she wouldn't be a nanny. It had seemed an easy job, but it held responsibility and, if they were told off all the time, not a happy one.

She pulled her shawl around her as a little black and white dog bounded up to her. She bent down to stroke it and looked around for its owner. Just then, a carriage came careering towards them, seemingly out of control, and Harriet thought the dog would be crushed beneath its wheels as it ran in front of it. "Stop," she cried, jumping up.

Fortunately, the driver controlled the horses, and reined them in a few inches away from her. He leaned over. "Are you hurt, miss?"

"No, thank God." Spotting the little dog bouncing up and down on the other side of the path, clearly unaffected, she sat down with a bump. The driver seemed satisfied, and the carriage continued on its way in a more sedate fashion.

So much for a peaceful morning.

Would the baby need feeding again? Missus Leekes had only mentioned giving him a little gruel or mashed potatoes, not whether she'd prepare them, or if she expected Harriet to, or when.

She checked inside the pram. The baby didn't seem to be breathing. With an intake of breath, she touched his cheek. Cold. Oh, no. "Please God don't let him be dead," she prayed. Even though she had only just met him, and had not the slightest idea what would happen when her parents returned, she still didn't want him dead. Everyone would say she was to blame. She didn't want to be labelled a murderess.

Then he stirred. "Phew. Thank you, God," she breathed. "Please don't do that again," she told the baby.

Deciding she had better go back and be around women who knew about babies, she adjusted her shawl and skirts and made her way back to Hare Street.

On the way, she saw two men, dressed in long, dirty coats and canvas trousers, squeezing themselves out of a grate in the road. They stank, even from that distance. One of them winked at Harriet as they approached, saying to the other, "Hey, Lanky Bill, don't she remind you o' your daughter?"

"Which one, One-Eyed, Jack? I got six."

"Haha, of course."

"Look what I found today." The man called Lanky Bill showed One-Eyed Jack something. Harriet couldn't see what it was, and didn't really want to know. It would probably stink as well.

"A whole sovereign. Some toff must have dropped it down the grate into the sewer."

"Cor blimey, mate. Are you sure it's real? You must feel like a millionaire."

"Of course it's real, and I do. This job ain't too bad, sometimes."

They passed by as Harriet held her nose. What possible job could they be doing, to find a whole sovereign? She had never even seen such a coin, and couldn't imagine how much it was worth.

Missus Bowe's front door stood wide open. Harriet popped her head inside and called, but received no reply. She wanted advice but would have to wait. Maybe Missus Leekes would be home. But she received the same response from that lady's house.

What if Tommy awoke and started crying? What could she feed him?

After leaving the pram outside, she had a rummage in the kitchen. Half a loaf of bread, would that do? Could babies eat bread? Maybe. Sausages? No. Surely he couldn't eat them with no teeth. Butter? That would be easy to swallow. After all, wasn't it made from milk? If push came to shove, she would give him that. She found a tin containing oats. As she poured some into a dish she racked her brain to remember how to make porridge. With milk and water, in a pan. The resulting gooey mess didn't look very appetising, but would the baby like it?

She went out to check on him and found him gurgling. "Hello, little boy," she greeted him as she lifted him out. "Aren't you a good baby? Not crying at all." With nobody in sight who might help her, she carried him indoors and sat him on the couch while she fetched his dinner. The bowl still felt hot. She didn't want to scald him. Only the other day she had put a spoonful of hot stew in her mouth and burned her tongue. "You don't want your tongue burning, do you?" she crooned, sticking her finger in the porridge to test it. Still too warm.

Tommy began to cry.

"No, no, please don't cry. It won't be long," she tried to pacify him. She put a little amount on the end of the spoon, and blew on it. "Here, see if you like it." He sucked on the spoon and yelled again. "Be patient. I can't put it all on at once," she cried as he slathered most of the food down his dress. "Oh, no, what can I mop it up with?" She grabbed the nearest thing to hand and was about to wipe him when she realised it was her mother's sewing. A dress for the new baby. She dropped it as if it had scalded her. A towel would be best. "Stay there," she warned as she ran into the kitchen to find one, but before she could grab anything, she heard a thud, and the baby's cry changed.

Chapter 6

Running back to the front room, she found Tommy face-down on the floor. She picked him up. No sign of blood. Phew! When he continued to cry down her lughole, she carried him into to the kitchen and found a clean towel. Then, after fetching his porridge, she sat on the chair and tried again. He swallowed the oaty mixture and she shovelled more into his mouth as quickly as she could.

However, when it had all gone, he continued to cry. "There's none left. I bet you're thirsty, aren't you. I'll see if I can find a baby's bottle. I'm sure there's one in the back of the cupboard."

Rummaging around with the baby in her arms proved tricky but, having taken out everything and leaving it on the floor, she found it. Even with both teats. "I'll have to put you down, though, Tommy, while I fill it. I'm not that clever." Trying to blot out his cries, she laid him on the rug - not wanting a repeat of his fall - took off one teat and quickly filled the bottle with cold water out of the kettle. Putting the teat back on, she raised it aloft with a cry of triumph. "Coming, Tommy, look what a clever girl I am."

He did not seem to want the water at first, but she persevered and he finished it. She held her breath in case he started bawling again, but he didn't. What an achievement. Tommy smiled. He thought so too.

It would be a different matter, though, changing his nappy. Missus Leekes had lent her a clean one. She laid him on the floor, undid the pin and took off the wet one, just as he decided to have a pee. A fountain shot up in the air, spraying all over his dress and the clean nappy lying beside him. "You little tinker," she cried, taking off his dress. "It's the only spare one, so you'll have to wear it wet." She tied the pin carefully, not wanting to poke him with it, and lifted him up. The nappy promptly fell off. "Um, that wasn't a good attempt, was it? Let's try again." After the third go, it stayed on. But she couldn't put the wet dress back on him. She'd have to find a clean one.

With a blanket around him, she carried him upstairs. He gave a loud burp, right in her ear. As she laughed, she noticed a bruise appearing on his forehead. He hadn't escaped unscathed, after all. She hoped it hadn't done any real damage. As he wasn't crying, hopefully it didn't hurt.

In her parents' bedroom she remembered the sound, and hoped she wouldn't hear it again. She laid Tommy on the bed and opened the top drawer. It revealed knickers and stockings. The bottom one came up trumps, containing a neatly folded pile of white baby clothes. She shook one out. "This'll do."

As if he could see someone, Tommy lay grinning at the ceiling at the very spot she had heard the noise. Her head jerked upwards, half of her expecting to see something there, the other dreading that she might. Still nothing. He kept on smiling, as if someone were talking to him. "Who is it, Tommy, eh? Is someone up there?" *Of course there can't be,* she told herself. Don't be stupid. What had her mother called her the day before? A will-o'-the-wisp. Well, maybe will-o'-the-wisps could see ghosts. But she couldn't see one.

He squirmed so much it took her ten minutes to dress him, but she finally pulled down the garment. It fitted perfectly. His little hands and feet were blue with cold, so she found a pair of bootees and a jacket. Happy when she also found a few nappies, she carefully rearranged the drawer and closed it.

After one last glance upwards she wrapped him in his shawl and went downstairs. "There you are, little Tommy, all warm and cosy. We'd better tidy up before Mama and Papa come home. They'll think a hurricane's landed." Tommy fell asleep on the couch as she did so. She cleared out the ashes in the hearth and lit a fire to ensure the room would be warm when they did return.

What would her mother say? And her father? He'd go mad, she felt sure. But what could she have done? Baby Tommy had been thrust upon her against her will. She couldn't abandon him. He was rather cute, and maybe she could grow to love him, as a sister, not as a mother-figure.

Had her brother survived? The officer had said he might not, but sometimes people did, against all the odds. Look at Mister Bowe. Everyone thought he would die, and he didn't. She had to hope for the best. Her mother always told her to do that, even though her father always looked on the negative side. He warned of doom and gloom all the time. If he were to be believed, the world would end before the turn of the century. But Queen Victoria would not allow that. She had been ruling the country for nearly sixty years.

Snuggling under a blanket, with Tommy's warm little body beside her, she fell asleep.

The baby's cries woke her. For a second, Harriet thought she was still in her dream, that she was in a stable, surrounded by sheep and cattle and donkeys, and that angels were proclaiming the birth of the Christ Jesus. Shepherds and kings were adoring the baby, who was lying in a manger, while a young girl…had it been her? Had she given birth to the saviour?

She blinked and rubbed her eyes, staring down at the baby beside her. Was he the new Jesus? Had she been chosen to be his mother? The priest had only said in his sermon the previous Sunday that He would come again one day. But how would she know? She hadn't had an apparition of angels. But maybe the noise she'd heard in her parents' bedroom had been an angel. And she'd ignored it. Dare she ask anybody? They would all laugh at her. Why would she be the chosen one? She wasn't a particularly holy person. She said her prayers night and morning, and tried to keep the commandments, but sometimes she had bad thoughts and did bad deeds, so bad she daren't confess them to the priest. Like the time she had seen someone drop a farthing in the street. Her conscience had told her to run after the woman, but she'd pocketed it and spent it little by little on sweeties and lollipops so nobody would be suspicious and ask her about it.

If she were to be the mother of the new Christ, she would have to improve. The Virgin Mary was sinless, and had been since birth. But perhaps God could not find such a girl for the second coming.

Anyway, whether he was the new Christ or not, the baby had a good pair of lungs and was screaming the place down. She scooped him up and hurried out, after dropping more coal on the fire, and damping it down, so it wouldn't burn out before her parents returned.

Missus Leekes stood at her doorway. "I thought I heard his cries," she declared as Harriet ran towards her. "He must be starving. Bring him in."

Chapter 7

While she watched him feed, Harriet wondered if she should voice her thoughts, but didn't know how to broach the subject. Anyway, Missus Leekes jabbered on about this and that and there never seemed to be a lull long enough for her to express herself. She'd been told that Isabel had gone for a walk to the park with a girl from up the street, and what she had been wearing, and how the girl had wanted to take John as well, but Missus Leekes had not thought her big enough to see over the perambulator handle. Blah, blah, blah.

John sat on the floor, playing with a rattle. She dropped down beside him, trying to compare his features with Tommy's. Did they look any different? Not really. He had bright blue eyes, whereas Tommy's were brown, but his nose and mouth were just the same. Jesus Christ looked ordinary, except he had a beard, and wore sandals. Babies didn't have beards, so that was no indication.

John whacked her on the head with his rattle. She laughed, although it had come keen, and she rubbed the spot.

"All done," declared Missus Leekes, buttoning her dress.

Harriet could smell stew cooking in the kitchen. It set her stomach rumbling, and made her wonder if she should prepare something for when her parents returned. Everything she did revolved around that thought. Maybe they already had. They wouldn't know where she was. She hadn't heard a carriage stop, but maybe they had walked. Not all the way from Hampshire, obviously, but from the train station.

She took Tommy and thanked Missus Leekes. Outside, she saw Isabel walking hand in hand with an older girl.

Isabel let go and ran towards her, putting her arms around Harriet's legs and hiding her face in her skirts.

"What's the matter?" Harriet asked, thinking something must be amiss.

"Nothing, I'm just happy to see you."

Did the child realise she was the mother of the new saviour? Nobody had ever greeted her as warmly. Maybe children could sense such things better than adults, for Missus Leekes hadn't seemed to notice.

"And I'm happy to see you as well. Did you have a nice walk?"

"Yes, but... Would you take me next time?"

"Very well, maybe on Saturday. I should go to school tomorrow."

"I'll be going to school in a little while."

The other girl stood quietly nearby. Her face didn't seem familiar. "Do you go to the school up the road?" Harriet asked, judging her to be about eleven.

She nodded, keeping her head down. "Sometimes. I started last week."

As Harriet opened her front door Isabel asked, "Can I come in your house?"

Wondering if her parents were inside, she didn't reply straightaway but, on seeing the house empty, she said she could.

"I'll be off, then," added the other girl.

"You may come in as well, if you like," replied Isabel, but then turned to Harriet. "She can, can't she?"

"I don't see why not. It's nice and warm in here." She put Tommy, who was still asleep, in the pram that she had managed to squeeze in behind the couch, and poked the fire, releasing a burst of flames.

Holding out her hands to the heat, she asked the girl her name.

"Frances," came the reply.

"And where do you live? I haven't seen you on this street before."

The girl pointed outside as if Harriet would be able to see where she meant. "We just moved in with me grandmamma, 'cos me pa died."

"I'm sorry. That must have been awful." Harriet couldn't imagine what that would be like.

"It was. He had that tubercolyostis."

"My uncle died from that," piped up Isabel, sitting on the rug, cross-legged.

"Who is your grandmamma?" asked Harriet, eager to find out on which side of the street she lived.

"Granma Betty."

That didn't help. "Where does she live?"

Frances pointed towards the window again. "Over there."

Ah, she meant the opposite side of the street, the unhealthy one. She didn't smell horrible, though.

Isabel jumped up. "Can I have a drink of water?"

"Of course. We'll all have one." Harriet's stomach rumbled again, and she took a glance at the clock. Four o'clock. No wonder it was almost dark. She lit a candle, carried it to the kitchen and poured them all a drink. Why were her parents taking so long? She didn't fancy spending another night at the Bowes' house. Soft and comfortable as Lucy's bed was, she would rather have her own. Lucy had kicked her several times during the night, and she didn't want to end up black and blue.

"Can we play a game," asked Isabel. "I like playing games."

"What can you play?"

"Snap."

"Very well. I'll fetch the cards, but don't shout too loud. We don't want to wake little Tommy."

"Where did he come from? Our John came out of ma's tummy."

"Well…" When she said she thought she was the chosen one, it sounded silly. Isabel and Frances looked at her with disbelief, and she laughed. "Only joking."

"Baby Jesus was born in a stable. Was Tommy?" asked Frances.

"I don't know where he was born."

The door opened and Missus Bowe poked her head around. "Are your parents home yet, Harriet?" she asked.

"No, Missus Bowe. I thought they would be. What could have happened to them?"

"Maybe your brother's still poorly. They know you're in my safe hands, and won't be worried." She glanced down at the other girls. "What's Isabel doing here, and who's this?"

"This is my new friend, Frances," answered Isabel. "She just moved here."

"Across the street?" When Frances nodded, Missus Bowe turned back to Harriet. "Are you sure your parents wouldn't mind?"

"Mind what?"

"Having a stranger in their house while they're not at home?"

"Why would they mind?"

The lady made a funny face, screwing up her eyes and shaking her head at Frances, as if trying to tell her something. What it was, Harriet couldn't fathom out.

"Just make sure everything's tucked away, if you know what I mean."

"Tucked away?" Harriet looked around the room. What needed tucking away? She's not long since tidied up.

Missus Bowe spoke to Frances. "Hadn't you better be off home now? It's dark outside."

Frances stood up as Isabel complained, "But we haven't finished our game."

"There'll be plenty of time tomorrow."

"But Harriet said she'd be going to school tomorrow."

"It doesn't look like it, now," replied Harriet. "Unless Mama and Papa arrive this evening."

"I expect your ma'll be wondering where you are, Isabel. You'd better go too." Missus Bowe shooed them out the door, warning them to go straight home, and then turned back inside, saying to Harriet, "You have to be careful, you know, with folk you don't know."

"I do know her. I met her this afternoon."

"She sounds foreign to me, and you can't always trust foreigners."

Harriet had not noticed any difference in the girl's speech. Maybe she said a few words differently, like she pronounced her name with an 'a' like in apple, instead of an 'ar' like in bath.

"I heard tell from one of my friends this morning that she and her mother used to live up north. A dodgy lot, them northerners. Even if they aren't foreigners, they're the next best thing. You need to make sure nothing valuable's left on view, if you know what I mean."

Why did she keep saying that? She had no idea what she meant. And, anyway, what valuables did they have? Her mother had a pair of dangly amethyst earrings that she kept wrapped up and hidden in a drawer upstairs. They had been her grandmother's, and she never wore them, in case she lost them, but sometimes took them out to show Harriet how well-off her grandparents had been. They would be Harriet's on her twenty-first birthday. She would probably not wear them, either. They were just an heirloom. Frances would not be rifling through her mother's drawers, even if she did live on the other side of the street, so the earrings were safe.

"Very well, Missus Bowe." Even though she couldn't understand why the lady was concerned, she agreed to be careful. "Will me and Tommy be able to stay at your house again tonight?" She had been about to suggest she stay at home, but remembered the noise upstairs. If the ghost, or angel, whatever it might be, appeared, she wouldn't know what to do.

"Yes, of course, my lovie. Do you want to come about six o'clock? Dinner will be ready by then." Harriet noticed the clock still said four o'clock. Surely it must be later than that. "I think the clock must have stopped. I forgot to wind it up last night. My pa usually does that. What time is it now?"

"It's about five. I'd better rush home, before Mister Bowe arrives. He don't like it if I'm not there when he comes in." As she hurried out, the candle spluttered.

"No, no, please don't go out before I find another one," Harriet begged as she dashed into the kitchen to find the box they kept under the sink. She grabbed a new one, and lit it as the old one went out. The fire had almost gone out as well; she put a few cobbles on it, thinking there wouldn't be much point putting on a lot. But what if her parents did return? Maybe a few more, just in case. They'd be chilled after their journey.

Tommy stirred and awoke. He lay contentedly, looking around. Her own little brother, Tommy, had cried a lot more. Not that she was complaining. Not at all.

Chapter 8

When Harriet found her parents had still not returned the next morning, she lit the fire that had gone out during the night.

Missus Leekes obligingly fed Tommy again, and seemed happy to continue, saying she had enough milk for an army. Why an army would want her milk, Harriet couldn't make out, but she was grateful. She didn't know what she'd have done without her.

Isabel tagged along with her as she returned home, and she wondered if Frances would call. Should she hide everything, like Missus Bowe had hinted? If her grandmother was the person Harriet thought she must be, she always looked smart, smarter than a lot of the people that lived on Hare Street, especially on the other side. Maybe it was a different grandmamma. Another old lady lived up on her own side, but she already had lots of family living with her, so it couldn't be her. She'd have to find out.

"Isabel, do you know exactly where Frances lives?"

"Um, no. With her gramma, didn't she say?"

"Yes, but which house?"

The little girl shrugged. "Please may we play cards again? I love playing games, but Ma's always too busy, and Pa's always too tired."

Harriet checked that Tommy had not woken and sat down next to her. "Very well, but not Snap. I'll teach you a new game. It's called Old Maid." She explained the rules and the little girl picked it up quickly. "You're clever, aren't you?"

"Yes, my pa always says that. He says I have the brains to be a brain surgeon or summat like that when I grow up."

"I agree. I need to decide what I'm going to do when I leave school. Mama says I ought to be working now, but my pa says I should finish my education first; that he earns enough money as a clerk down at the docks, together with the sewing Mama takes in." She told Isabel about the nanny she had met the previous day. "I don't want to be miserable, like her, so I'm not going to be one of them."

They finished the game. Isabel won. "May we play again?"

"I suppose so." Harriet drew back the curtain to look for any sign of a carriage stopping, or anyone passing who resembled her mother and father. It had started snowing. That would hinder their return even further.

She opened the door, letting in a blast of cold air.

Isabel jumped up and joined her, clapping her hands in glee. "Goodie, I love snow. We can build a snowman."

"I do usually, but how will Mama and Papa find their way home if it falls heavily?"

Isabel stared up at her with concern in her eyes. "You miss them, don't you?"

"Yes, of course I do. They've never left me before. Even when we went with William to take him to his new place, they took me with them."

"Is he dead? My ma says he is."

"I really don't know. For their sake, I hope not. But if he is, why aren't they home?" She closed the door and kicked the tapestry draught-excluder back into place.

"The baby's awake." Isabel poked him in the cheek. "May I play with him?"

Harriet took him out of the pram and sat with him on the rug. She hadn't realised he could sit on his own.

Isabel tickled him under his chin and he giggled. "Ah, ain't he lovely!" she proclaimed, repeating the action. "Our John don't do that."

"Yes, he's a little treasure, the…" She had been about to say the new Jesus, but the more she thought about the idea, the less likely it seemed. Maybe she should change his name to Jesus, then everybody would realise, and it would make it

more obvious. "What do you think about the name Jesus?" she asked, to test the water.

"Jesus came to save us, my ma says."

"Yes, he did, but…" Never mind. She would just call him Jesus in her mind for the time being. She searched his face for any indication that he might be a saviour, but it looked normal. Two eyes, a nose and a mouth. No teeth, as far as she could see, but she knew babies didn't have them at first. In fact, their Tommy never did have any.

"Can he walk?" asked Isabel, lifting him to his feet.

Grabbing him before the child dropped him, she replied, "I don't think he can, but I hadn't known he could sit up on his own." She held him under his arms and stood him up.

"If you let go, you'll find out," suggested Isabel.

She tried it, but he fell.

"Phaw, he whiffs. He needs his nappy changing. My ma says our John can shit for England some days."

Harriet gasped. "She doesn't use words like that, does she? And you shouldn't."

"What? England? Why not?"

Harriet couldn't bring herself to use what she considered a swear word. "No, silly, the other word."

"My ma says it all the time. Shi…"

Harriet jerked forward and covered the baby's ears. "Stop it, it's swearing. If my mama comes in and hears you saying that, she'll tan your backside."

Isabel began to cry. "I didn't mean no harm."

"Well, please don't say it again, or you won't be allowed to come here any more."

"I'm sorry. Please let me stay."

"Very well, but only if you're on your best behaviour." Harriet undid the nappy pin. "Phaw, you were right. He does stink. Hold that leg while I clean him up."

"What do you call it, then, Harriet?" The little girl held her nose with one hand, trying to stop Tommy kick his feet in the mess with the other.

"It isn't spoken about, but I say 'big jobs'."

"Big jobs?" the little girl laughed and repeated it. "Big jobs."

"Anyway, I'll be running out of nappies. I'd better wash these." The baby propped up by cushions, she ordered Isabel to watch him while she went to the wash house where she filled the boiler and lit it.

Minutes later, she heard a cry and saw Isabel dragging Tommy through the door by his arms. "What on earth are you doing?" she yelled.

"He was crying and I couldn't carry him."

With a sigh, she picked him up and examined him. Apart from the purple bruise and a dirty and slightly-ripped dress, he seemed fine. "I hope I can find another one," she moaned as a voice came from outside, and her next-door neighbour came into the wash house.

"I thought I heard you out here," she said, showing her one black front tooth. "How are you managing? I gather your parents aren't home yet?"

"I'm managing quite well most of the time, and no, they aren't."

"If you need any clothes, just speak up. I have a drawer-full upstairs that I've been saving in case I have another bairn."

Harriet knew the lady was Scottish, and used odd words, like 'bairn' and 'awa' instead of 'away'. "If they fit, I'd be very grateful," she replied.

The neighbour took the baby. "Would you mind if I looked after him for a while? My youngest boy, Mark, is ten now, and I miss having a baby to cuddle."

"Ah, thank you, Missus Edwards, that would be wonderful. As you see, I have his nappies and clothes to wash." Harriet rolled up her sleeves, the heat from the

boiler already making her warm. "His perambulator is in the front room, if you want to take that."

Isabel looked up as if to say something, but was forestalled by Missus Edwards. "No, no. I just want a cuddle. I'll bring him back when I've had enough."

When she had gone out, Isabel said, "You shouldn't have let her take him. She murdered her own baby."

"That's not true. He died, that's all."

"Well, my ma says she did."

"And my ma says she didn't, so there. Pass me that towel. I may as well wash that too." She didn't have time to argue with little girls who didn't know what they were talking about. Of course the woman hadn't murdered her baby. As if she would! If she loved babies enough to borrow Tommy, she couldn't have. And, anyway, if he were the son of God, he would have to grow up before he could start saving souls. Should she have warned Missus Edwards from next door about that? Too late. Maybe next time.

After scrubbing the dirty nappies with soap on the washboard, she ran the clothes through the mangle, urging Isabel to keep well clear. An accident, such as one she'd had the year before, when she had caught her finger in it and taken off her fingernail, would be the last straw.

Now she had the problem of drying it. Would there be any point in hanging it out? She nudged a grim-faced, sullen Isabel out of the way, and went outside to check. Compared with the heat in the washroom, the air had a distinct chill to it. Luckily the snow had not come to anything. Clouds scudded across the sky, some of them menacing-looking, but she may as well try. Perhaps the sun would come out later. She asked Isabel to pass the pegs while she hung the clothes on the line. The child still seemed out of sorts, but if she were not happy she could always go home. Nobody was forcing her to stay. Much as she enjoyed her company, even though she was only little, she didn't want her in a miserable mood.

45

Isabel soon cheered up when a little grey kitten wandered onto the back yard from down the ginnel that separated their house from next door. She bent down to stroke it. "Ah, ain't it sweet?"

"I hope it doesn't have fleas."

The child jerked her hand and tried to shoo the animal away. "My ma says fleas are dirty creatures. Missus next-door had them. They jump." She tried to imitate one, jumping in the air, with her little legs tucked under her.

The washing finished, Harriet went to the front again, to look for a carriage. One or two of the newfangled bicycle contraptions drove past, a few horses and one or two carriages that didn't stop. Couldn't they have sent word to her as to their intentions?

Missus Leekes came up the street, pushing her baby in his pram. "Isabel, are you coming home? Are you behaving yourself?"

With a worried face, Isabel looked up at Harriet as if to ask her opinion.

"Yes, Missus Leekes," Harriet spoke up for the child. "She's been a big help."

"We saw a cute little kitten, Ma. It was really soft."

"Well, I hope it didn't have fleas."

"Exactly what I said, Missus Leekes," added Harriet, giving the girl a smug look from under her eyebrows. "You can't be too careful, can you?"

"I know many of the houses across the street are infested, but we don't want them hopping over to our side."

"No, no."

"Where's the baby? I gather you still have him, or has his mother reclaimed him?"

Isabel pulled her mother down to whisper loudly in her ear, "She lent him to…" she nodded her head towards the neighbour's door, "to that lady who…"

Missus Leekes' eyes opened wide as she realised the implication of her words. "You mean…the murderess?" she mouthed the last word, clearly not wanting the lady in question to hear her.

"See," cooed Isabel, "I told you."

"Well, my ma says the baby just died, and I'd rather believe her. No mother would kill her own baby. It isn't possible." Shivering, Harriet turned to go inside, not having had the foresight to put on her coat. As she did so, the rumble of wheels on the cobble stones could be heard. "They're here. It must be them." Wrapping her arms around her body, she waited. Missus Leekes picked up Isabel and they stood in a state of anticipation until the carriage passed by without stopping.

"Wait," called Harriet. "Stop." But it continued to the other end and turned the corner. "Why didn't it stop? Why weren't my ma and pa in it?" Tears rolled down her cheeks at the disappointment. She had been managing up until then, but the excitement of thinking they had returned had changed to desolation in the space of a few minutes.

Missus Leekes put down her daughter and placed her arm around Harriet's shoulder. "There, there, lovie. I'm sure they won't stay away much longer. Come to my house and I'll make you a nice cup of tea."

Harriet allowed herself to be steered away, after grabbing hers and Isabel's coats and closing her door.

Over a welcome cup of strong tea, made with milk, Harriet said, "I mustn't stay long because Missus Edwards from next door won't know where I am when she wants to bring Tommy back." After another of Isabel's creased brows, she added, "Do you really think she killed her baby, Missus Leekes?"

"Well…" The lady stroked her chin. "Well, that's what people say. She was never convicted, or she'd be in prison now, or even worse, sent to that awful place where they

47

chain them up and make them break up rocks and things 'til they die."

Harriet laughed. "You mean Australia? We learnt about it in school."

"They teach you some peculiar things in that school. I'm sure I never learnt anything like that. Mind you, I never went," Missus Leekes chuckled, "so it stands to reason, don't it? Haha."

Isabel looked up from the floor where she was playing with her dolls. "I'm going to school soon, ain't I, Ma?"

"Yep, I hope you learn more than I did. There weren't really any proper schooling when I were a girl."

John began to cry, and she picked him up and unbuttoned her blouse.

"I'd better be going," said Harriet. "Thank you for the tea. I'll see if Missus Edwards from next door has had enough of Baby Je... I mean Tommy." Should she confide in Missus Leekes? She seemed sympathetic. But she wanted her mother to be the first to find out.

"Why do you call her Missus Edwards from next door all the time?" asked Isabel, her face screwed up in a frown.

"Because there used to be another Missus Edwards across the road. She's dead now. Ma called her Missus Edwards from the other side and our neighbour Missus Edwards from next door."

Satisfied, Isabel returned to her dolls.

It started to snow again as Harriet made her way home. The washing would never dry. It hung on the line, limp and lifeless, covered in large snowflakes. With a sigh, she fetched it all in to hang on the clothes horse, and stoked up the fire. Steam soon rose. Her mother hated washing in the house, but needs must.

She sunk onto the couch, imagining what could happen if her parents didn't return soon. She had no money, hardly any food apart from the dinner she was to prepare for them and a few jars of pickles her mother had made in the

summer, when fruit had been plentiful. And not a lot of coal. How would she buy more? She would have to scrounge a few cobbles off the neighbours, and pay them back when she could.

In tears again, she picked up a photograph of her parents on their wedding day. Her mother had told her it had cost an arm and a leg, even though her brother had taken it. In those days, photography had been a new occupation, but her uncle had started at the right time, and made a good living from it, until he had died from that awful tuberculosis that had killed Frances's father. "Dear Mama, dear Papa, please come home soon," she whispered as she kissed their faces and hugged the picture to her bosom.

Chapter 9

About to go next door to fetch Tommy, she felt a draught of cold air when the door opened, as if by magic. Probably Missus Edwards from next door had come to her instead. But no, not her at all. A shriek escaped her when she recognised the white beard and sparkling brown eyes of her grandfather, "Gampy!" She ran to him and he enfolded her in his big arms.

"That's the sort of welcome I enjoy," he murmured in his deep voice, seemingly as affected by the reunion as she. He tried to ease her away, but wanting to stay there forever, she clung on to his smelly oilskin. "Eh, my girl, what's the matter? Come on now, let's be having a goosy gander at you. My, how you've grown since the last time I was home."

She obeyed and took his weather-beaten hand and kissed the back of it. "Oh, Gampy, I'm so pleased to see you. You'll never believe what's happened."

"Well, put the kettle on and you can tell me over a hot cup of rosy lee." He took off his outer clothes and hung them on the hook on the back of the door. "Where's your mother?"

"That's part of what I'll be telling you," she replied as she made the tea, taking in his much-loved face, his roman nose, and those kindly brown eyes. "Sit yourself down and I'll begin."

"I suppose you're too big now to sit on my knee while I tell you a hope and glory, a story," he chuckled. "But not big enough for me to sit on your knee."

She laughed aloud. "My wonderful Gampy. You don't know how much I've missed you and your rhymes."

"I've missed you more, all those days at sea. Anyway," he took a sip of his drink, "fire away."

Having told him everything that had happened, when she came to the part about baby Tommy, she hesitated. Should she mention her fears—for that was what they were—that he might be the Messiah? Might as well go the whole hog.

"Child…" His head to one side when she had explained, he looked into her eyes. "I don't think so. After all, isn't the Messiah supposed to come on a cloud the next time? That's what I learnt at my mother's knee."

"I knew it really. I kept telling myself it couldn't be, that I'm not good enough. Anyway, I don't have the right name. Even my second name is Alice, like my ma's, not Mary."

He nodded as he finished his tea and poured himself another cupful. "So, you have no far and near when they'll be back, my daughter and your pa?"

With a shake of her head, she added, "No, no idea at all. And it's snowing. They'll never get through that if it gets deep." She stood up. "Shall I cook you a nice dinner, Gampy? I'm sure you must he hungry."

"What do you have?"

"Well…" She took the lid off the saucepan containing the vegetables she and her mother had prepared. "Oo, they don't look very good. They're all slimy. I'll look in the pantry to see if we have any more."

Opening the meat safe, she smelled the sausages. Not too bad, with no mouldy patches. There were enough fresh vegetables for two of them, even taking into consideration her grandfather's hearty appetite.

"Sausages all right, Gampy?" she called. When she received no reply, she backed out. Her grandfather had been sitting on the kitchen chair, but had moved.

She found him asleep in the armchair, covered him with a blanket and returned to the kitchen to prepare the meal. Should she fetch baby Tommy? He rarely cried, and wouldn't wake Gampy. If Missus Edwards from next door had had enough of him, she'd have brought him back. But

51

what if Isabel was right? Wiping her hands down her apron, she rushed out and, without knocking, raced inside her neighbour's house, calling, "Missus Edwards, are you there?" No reply. No sign of anyone. Not even her son, Mark. She took a quick look around and called upstairs again, deciding she must have taken Tommy for a walk.

At least it had stopped snowing, and what had settled earlier had melted. Something was going her way.

Gampy still snoozing, she checked the dinner. The sausages had burnt on one side. Biting her lip, she turned them over and poured more water into the saucepan of vegetables that had boiled over. Should she wake him when it was ready? And should she ask him for money? It would be awful if her parents arrived after their long journey, starving and hungry—*although they mean the same thing,* she chuckled to herself—and there was no food left.

Sticking a fork in the potatoes, she decided they were cooked. Gampy slept on. Her stomach rumbled. But she couldn't start without him. That would be the height of bad manners. She put the saucepan to the outside of the range and forked the sausages onto the plates. It wouldn't matter if they cooled. They looked so tempting, sitting there. Gampy wouldn't know how many she'd cooked. After all, if they'd eaten them the day she'd bought them, there would have been enough for her and her parents. Knowing how partial her grandfather was, she'd cooked them all, for they wouldn't have lasted another day. She could always have just one with her dinner, instead of the two she had intended.

The temptation too strong, she rammed one into her mouth and bit off a chunk. Delicious. She chewed slowly, savouring the spicy flavour, her eyes rolling around in delight.

"I hope that isn't one of mine," came a voice from behind her.

She swivelled round, the half-eaten sausage in mid-air.

"Caught in the act, young lady." However, the glint in her grandfather's eyes told her he was joking.

Swallowing quickly, she put the remains of the little bag of mystery on the plate. Her mother called them that, because she said you never knew what went into them. They tasted so good she didn't care what they were made from.

The meal finished, Harriet washed the dishes, trying to pluck up the courage to ask her grandfather for money, knowing the shopkeeper would not allow her tick, as the bill had to be paid on Fridays, and her father wasn't there to collect his wages, let alone pay any bills.

However, Gampy looked in the pantry for cake for his dessert. "You'd better fetch a few supplies, girl." He felt around in his trouser pocket and brought out a battered old, brown wallet. "Here, treat yourself to some sweeties as well, while I nip up the apples and pears and unpack. Do you have enough heart and soul for the fire?"

She shook her head.

"Call at the coal merchants then, and order a bag."

She raised herself onto her tiptoes and kissed his furry cheek. "Thank you, Gampy. I'll be as quick as I can, and I'll pop and tell Missus Bowe that you're back."

Skipping down the street, she couldn't keep the grin from her face. Good old Gampy. What would she have done without him and his rhyming slang?

Chapter 10

The pantry stocked, and coal to be delivered the following day, Harriet and her grandfather sat down with a warming drink of cocoa.

"I'll check with Missus Edwards from next door again in a minute, to see if she's had enough of the baby," she said, not at all eagerly.

"You don't want to be saddled with a baby, my girl, not at your age." Her grandfather took out his pipe and lit it. The smoke smelled so much sweeter than Mister Bowe's.

"Well, if Mama doesn't agree... After all, she'll have her own soon, so two babies..."

Gampy sat up and leaned forward. "You didn't tell me my daughter was expecting."

"Oo, I'm sorry. With everything else happening I must have forgot."

He leaned back. "Well, well."

"I named the foundling after Tommy."

"That was nice. But won't your ma want to name her baby after his big brother, if she has a boy?"

She bit her lip. "I never thought of that. But maybe she'll have a girl, so I'll have a sister."

Shrugging, he banged his pipe in the fire. "I think I'll go down to the Princess for a pig's ear. I'll see you later."

"Goodbye, Gampy. Don't get...what's the word you use for drunk? Brahms and Liszt?"

"Well, a well-brought up young lady would not use that expression, my dear, but no, I won't." He pulled on his oilskin and, chuckling, scooted out.

Harriet went out the back. Her nose pinched with one hand against the stench, she lifted her dress with the other. Even though it was too short, she didn't want to soil it as she pushed her way through her neighbour's pigs.

Missus Edwards from next door was singing to the baby as she tapped on the door and entered.

"Ah, my dear, I didn't expect you so soon," declared the lady, cuddling him to her bosom. "I can't tell you how much I've enjoyed looking after him." Harriet could only stare at her black front tooth. Why didn't she have it taken out? It looked odd, stuck there on its own. It dawned on her that the lady had continued talking, and was asking if she could keep him. "Keep him? What, for good, do you mean?"

"I been desperate for another baby for the last few years, but God ain't seen fit to bestow one on me. This little one seems like a gift from heaven."

"Do you really think so?" Could Missus Edwards tell he was the new Messiah? But she rarely went to church. "All babies are gifts from heaven, Missus Edwards," she replied, stalling, because she couldn't make up her mind if she wanted him or not. Like her grandfather had said, she was too young to be saddled with him, and would her mother be prepared to have him?

The lady picked up the baby under his armpits and looked into his eyes. "I agree. Of course they are, but this baby seems extra special."

"So you do realise it?"

Her neighbour gave her a funny look from under her brows. "Is there something you're not telling me? What did his mother say when she handed him over?"

"Um, she asked if Bill was home, and when I said we don't have anyone called Bill at our house, she just bunged him in my arms."

"But your grandfather's called Bill, isn't he?"

Puffing out her cheeks, she tried to work out what the lady meant. "Are you saying Gampy might be the baby's father? No, Missus Edwards, that can't be possible. Of course not. Anyway, he's been away at sea for months." She made as if to take the baby from her, but the woman clung onto him and swivelled round with her back to her.

"Please, let me keep him. I promise if your grandfather wants him, I'll hand him over, but until then... Please allow me to look after him for you."

At that moment the son, Mark, came downstairs. His mother cried, "Marky, we can have him, for a little while, anyway. Isn't that wonderful?"

The boy s bottom lip jutted out and he turned and went back upstairs without speaking.

"You will take really, really good care of him, won't you?" asked Harriet, trying to think of a way she could bring up the accusations that Isabel and her mother had mentioned. "You won't let him...um...die?"

"Why on earth would I do that?" A light seemed to come on in her brain. "Ah, you've heard what people say, have you?" Harriet nodded. "Well, rest assured I did not kill my child. He died in his sleep. There didn't seem anything wrong with him. He hadn't had any illness and I didn't do nothing to him. He just...died."

Her eyes filled with tears and she rocked Tommy in her arms, looking tenderly into his face.

Harriet believed her. How could she not? The woman seemed genuine. She patted her arm. "I'll let you know when my parents are home."

Missus Edwards nodded, so Harriet went home, determined to allay everybody's fears about the woman. "In fact, I'll go right away and tell Missus Leekes what you said."

As she went up the street she hoped God would not mind her giving the baby away. After all, Gampy had said it couldn't be possible for him to be the new Messiah, so it made sense for a lady who really wanted him to have him.

Missus Leekes didn't seem convinced when she told her what had happened. "Well, lovie, there's no smoke without fire," she pronounced as Harriet sat on the floor to help Isabel complete her jigsaw.

"But there wasn't a fire, or anything like that. He just died."

"People don't just die, my dear, even babies. There has to be a reason."

Harriet watched her change John's nappy, feeling as if a weight had been lifted from her shoulders with the departure of baby Tommy. Much as she loved him she couldn't be more grateful that she wouldn't have to worry about doing such a smelly job again.

"Good news: Gampy arrived home today," she declared.

"That's good. You won't be on your own any more." She hadn't been on her own before, she'd had Tommy for company, but thought better of arguing with the lady.

"Who's Gampy?" asked Isabel, breaking up the finished jigsaw.

"He's my ma's father, and he's been away at sea for a long time," she explained. "Sometimes he brings me a present, but he hasn't done this time. Unless he forgot to give it me before he went to the alehouse." Harriet stood up. "I'll be going now, then." She looked at Isabel to see if she'd give any hint that she might want to go with her, but the little girl took out another toy. Clearly, she was still out of sorts with her.

Outside, she saw Lucy ahead and hurried to catch up.

"My grandfather's home and more good news, Missus Edwards from next door has asked to keep baby Tommy, so I don't have to worry about him any more."

Lucy's eyes opened wide.

Harriet stopped her before she could speak. "Now, don't say what everybody else thinks. I don't believe she can be a murderess. She seems to truly love him, giving him cuddles, and kissing him all the time."

They arrived at the Bowe's house and Lucy opened the door. "Well, on your head be it. Are you coming in for a while?"

Harriet looked up and down the street, just in case. No carriage. "Um, no thank you, maybe tomorrow. Will you be at work?"

"Yes, but not on Sunday. After you've been to church we could go somewhere."

"We'll see. It all depends on…"

"Of course. Goodbye." Lucy closed the door behind her and Harriet rubbed her chilblained hands to warm them.

Arriving home, she gave a yelp of glee on seeing her mother warming herself in front of the fire. "Mama, thank goodness you're home. I have such a tale to tell you."

Her mother turned with tears in her eyes and hugged her tightly. She had never been a demonstrative woman and had never hugged her that hard before, but Harriet didn't mind. She hugged her back. After a minute or so, with no let up, she squirmed. "Where's Papa?" she asked, easing herself away.

"He…" She opened her reticule. Taking out a handkerchief, she blew her nose and dabbed her streaming cheeks. "He…" she began again. "Oh, Harriet, my darling girl, it was so awful. I can't begin to explain."

Harriet looked around the room for any sign of him, but could only see her mother's reticule, not even the tapestry bag they had taken. But maybe that had been taken upstairs already.

"Is William Henry dead?"

Sniffing, her mother nodded.

She had been expecting that, so why did she feel so bad? "Has Papa stayed with him?" she asked as tears ran down her face.

"Sit down, child, I have even worse news, if things could be worse than my only son being dead, killed needlessly in a freak accident."

All sorts of ideas swum around her brain, but nothing like what her mother whispered. "Your papa also."

"What? My papa is also what? You can't mean dead?"

Her mother nodded, sniffing once more into her handkerchief. "Yes, he was that upset when we arrived too late to see William, he wasn't thinking straight, and fell off a bridge into a river and drowned."

"No! You must be wrong."

"The funerals are tomorrow, both together, at Bow Cemetery."

This could not be happening. She must be dreaming again, and would wake up and laugh at the silliness of her dream. She blinked, trying to change the situation, but her mother still sat there on the sofa, wringing her hands, staring at the floor. Compassion for her mother overtook her own feelings. "Why did you not call for me to join you? That must have been awful, on your own."

Her mother did look at her then. "I... there wasn't time, and I didn't want to bother you."

"Bother me, Mama? I'm nearly fourteen. I could have supported you."

"Anyway, it's too late now."

Harriet jumped up. "I'll find Gampy. He's back from sea and has gone to the Princess."

Her mother's face lit up. "How wonderful. I'll come with you."

Before they could leave, though, Missus Edwards from next door called from the kitchen. "Coee, is that you, Freda?"

"Yes, Mary."

Harriet had forgotten Missus Edwards from next door's name was Mary. How appropriate, if she were to keep the baby. She hadn't had time to explain the situation to her mother, and this was definitely not the right moment. She raced through to prevent the lady coming in and spilling the beans. Speaking in hushed tones, she appraised her of her mother's dilemma, not going into detail about how it had happened.

"Oh, my God," exclaimed Missus Edwards from next door.

"So we're going to find my grandfather."

"Yes, yes. Give your mother my deepest sympathies. And don't you worry about the baby. He'll be just fine with me."

Harriet urged her out the back door. "Thank you, Missus Edwards."

Her mother stood on the front doorstep. "What did she want?"

"Nothing much, Mama. She sends her deepest sympathies."

Her mother nodded as they went out. "I suppose the whole street will know within a short while. At least it'll save me having to tell everyone individually."

They reached The Princess and stopped outside.

"We can't go in," said her mother, peeping through the door. "Just listen to that noise." The place was indeed raucous, with laughter and ribaldry streaming out through the chink her mother had created.

"Shall we ask this...?" Harriet had been about to say 'gentleman', but on further inspection of the person approaching she decided to call him what he was. "This man to go in and ask for Gampy, I mean Mister Bond?"

"I don't know..."

"I'll do it."

She took a deep breath as he drew level.

"Good day, ladies," the man declared in a surprised tone of voice. "You're not the usual ladies we have in our establishment." He pronounced the word 'ladies' in a derogatory way.

"No, sir," replied Harriet, unsure what sort of ladies they might be, but not in the mood to ask. "Please would you be so kind as to see if Mister William Bond is inside?"

"Old Bill, is he home from his travels?"

"Yes, sir. Would you…?" She indicated with her head towards the door.

The man put on an affected accent. "Seeing has how you har hasking me so nicely, I shall do has you request. Who might I say his requesting his presence?"

"For goodness sake, man, get on with it," cried her mother, clearly running out of tolerance.

The man pulled a face and opened the door, muttering, "Yes, ma'am, sorry ma'am."

They paced up and down the road, waiting for what seemed like ages before her grandfather appeared. "Freda, Harriet!" He seemed to sense that something was amiss, and continued, "I'll fetch my coat," as he hurried inside, reappearing moments later. "I couldn't Adam and Eve it when Pete said there were two lovely ladies asking for me. But I sense you're not here to stop me getting Brahms and Liszt."

"No, Gampy."

"I'll tell you when we're indoors," added her mother. "I don't want the whole neighbourhood knowing my business, although, for certain, they'll find out before long."

Gampy gave Harriet a look behind her mother's back and she shook her head. His brown eyes turned sad, even though he couldn't possibly imagine what he'd be about to hear.

"I'll put the kettle on," she declared when they had hung up their coats and her mother had sunk onto the armchair.

He followed her into the kitchen. "Well?" he asked, putting his arms around her.

"Oh, Gampy." She rested her head on his shoulder, her favourite place of refuge. "But let Mama tell you. Sit with her while I do this."

She went to the pantry to fetch the milk. The butter dish holding the butter she had bought for her father sat staring at her. She broke down, knowing he would never taste it. After wiping her eyes, so her mother wouldn't be upset by her emotion, she took a deep breath and carried in the tray.

Her mother had already begun the story. How they had arrived a mere hour after William Henry had gone to heaven, and how he'd never regained consciousness after being shot in the chest. It had been a stupid, senseless prank by his fellow soldiers. One of them had been bragging about his brilliant showmanship with a gun, and somehow, it had gone off, and William had been in the firing line. The other two men were to be court-marshalled and would probably receive the death penalty.

Harriet gasped. "But, they wouldn't have intended any harm? Isn't that too severe?"

"That's what I thought," her mother continued. "But they have to show an example. Anyway, your father went mad. He broke down, sobbing as if his heart was broken. It was pitiful to see him. Much as I wanted to do the same, I had to support him. The officer who had been explaining what had happened didn't know what to do. He was only a young man. I felt sorry for him."

Gampy took her hands in his. "That shows what a marvellous lady you are, my dear. Even in the face of your own desolation, you found the strength in your heart to show sympathy for a stranger. But where is Thomas?"

"He…" She broke down, unable to continue.

Gampy looked at Harriet for the answer.

"He isn't coming home either, Gampy. He fell in a river."

"Fell in a river?"

62

Her mother still sobbing, Harriet had to explain something she didn't understand herself. "That's all I know. Mama said he fell in a river and drowned."

He sat staring into space, wiping his hands across his beard. "So are they bringing the coffins tonight?" he eventually asked.

Her mother tried to compose herself. "No, I didn't know what time I'd arrive home, and I couldn't let them come here with Harriet on her own—I didn't know you were here, of course." She turned to Harriet. "What a shock that would have been for you, my dearie."

"Yes, it would, but couldn't they have brought you with them?"

"No, my child. So, we'll have to forgo the...whatever one would call it, certainly not pleasure...of watching over them tonight." She stood up. "I need to start preparing for the wake. It's too late to buy anything now, but there are pickles in the pantry. I shall have to go first thing in the morning." She stopped and looked at Harriet. "Will you sleep with me tonight, my dear? I don't want to be alone."

"Yes, of course, Mama."

Chapter 11

Harriet crept out of bed quietly, so as not to disturb her mother. Gampy had already been to the shop, and she helped him make sandwiches and set out plates of ham and trimmings.

"Take your ma a cup of rosie lee," Gampy said when they were satisfied they had prepared everything, but she came down as Harriet put her foot on the bottom stair.

"You are good," her mother exclaimed. As she drank her tea, Harriet whispered to her grandfather, "Do you think we should tell her now about..." She indicated towards next door.

"What are you whispering about?" asked her mother.

"Mama, we have something else to tell you."

Between them they told her about the baby.

"But you say the woman asked for Bill?" she asked aghast.

"The only Bill here is me, and I sure ain't the baby's father," muttered Gampy, relieving Harriet's fears. "The mother must have got the wrong address."

"Yes, that must be it. But Missus Edwards from next door is happy to keep Tommy until we decide what to do." Harriet sat beside her.

"You poor child, having all that to cope with on your own." She enfolded Harriet in her arms. "I'm so sorry. What's he like, this baby?"

"His name's Tommy."

"How fitting." She smiled. "Did the mother tell you that?"

"No, Mama, she never told me anything. That's just what I've called him, after our Tommy. But Gampy says you might want to call the new baby Tommy, so I can change it if you do."

"No, dearie. Anyway, I think this little one will be a girl."

"Do you? How can you tell?"

"Just a feeling." She pressed her belly as a look of pain covered her face. "Anyway, the undertakers will be here any time now. Oh, Papa, how will we bear it?"

"I'll be there for you." He stroked the back of her hand. "And I've been thinking. It's time I gave up my wayward ways, and stopped sailing the high seas. I shall stay at home and look after you both, well, all three of you."

Her mother looked into his brown eyes. "You'd do that for us?"

Harriet put her arms around him. "Gampy, that'd be a real sacrifice."

"No, it wouldn't. I can't Adam and Eve I didn't think of it before."

She smiled. "I wondered how you'd managed to complete a whole morning without rhyming. But, are you sure?"

"Never surer, my dears, never surer. I have a small amount of bread and honey I've stashed away over the years, so we'll muddle along."

"I was so worried we'd have to move away, but where would we go? There can't be many houses with such cheap rents anywhere in London. I know it isn't the best street but..."

"But it's the only street I've ever lived in," Harriet completed the sentence for her. "My friends are here. I couldn't bear the thought of moving away."

"Well, my dear..." began her grandfather, pulling the curtain to one side. "Never mind that now. The what could be worse is pulling up outside, if I'm not mistaken."

"I beg your pardon?" Harriet pushed past him to see what he meant. "Gampy, you mean the hearse. I swear you make up some of those rhymes."

"Please excuse you. I'll see you later. I need to go."

"Wait for me," cried Harriet, pulling her coat from the hook.

"You can't go to the funeral, neither can your mother. Women don't."

"Why not?"

"It's…" He stroked his beard. "It's just not the done thing."

Harriet looked at her mother. "Mama?"

"Well, I'm going whether it's right or wrong. You can make up your own mind, Harriet."

"I'm coming too. They are my family. I can't desert them now."

Gampy shook his head as they filed outside and he stood with his hat in his hand, head bowed. Harriet squeezed her mother's arm as neighbours came out to pay their respects. The coffins—one plain and the other draped with the national flag and William Henry's sword and sash—lay on the backs of two carts, each drawn by a mangy black horse. Harriet thought her mother could have hired a better-looking pair, but perhaps they were all she could afford.

They took their places behind them, followed by what seemed like the whole street. She had thought a few might attend, but hadn't bargained for that many. Hopefully, they wouldn't all come back to the house. There wouldn't be enough food to feed them all.

More and more people joined the line of mourners, and others stood in their doorways, hats in hands; out of Hare Street and through Bethnal Green towards the church.

As they approached Mile End, Harriet felt her mother wince and heard her mumble. "Are you well?" she whispered, glancing at her.

Her mother nodded.

After the short church service, in which William Henry's achievements were highlighted—how he had been head boy at school, captain of his house and then captain of

66

his school, Harriet recalled the fancy cap he wore, with a tassel to show for his efforts, and bit the inside of her cheek to stop herself breaking down.

Arriving at the grave side, Harriet felt her mother wince again. Gampy took her arm and led her and Harriet to the other side of the open hole as other mourners spread around it. It was not as if her father had been particularly popular. He was a stickler for good manners and kept himself to himself, apart from the times when he would have a pint or two in his favourite alehouse, The Old George. Several of his drinking friends could be seen across from them.

Harriet looked at her mother with wonder. How serene she seemed and composed, although every now and again she would look up with a peculiar face, but not at all sad. Shouldn't she be weeping into her handkerchief? She herself was trying not to, even though she had brought one, especially. The collar of her black dress irritated her. The dress was too small, but they had not had time to buy another.

"Dust to dust, ashes to ashes," droned the priest.

Her feet hurt, the left one more than the right. Maybe she'd tied the lace too tightly. Dare she bend down and loosen it? Better not. It would only draw attention to herself. She'd have to grin and bear it. Having something else to concentrate on took away part of the pain in her heart.

Glancing at the faces around her, she felt sure she would see her father standing there, not dead at all. And William Henry. That would be his sort of jape, to pretend to be dead and pop up at the last minute and shout, "Boo! Had you for a minute, didn't I?" They hadn't had the chance to see the bodies, so maybe someone had got it wrong. Maybe those men inside the coffins were someone else's loved ones.

Her grandfather handed her a box of soil, and she took out a few grains and threw them into the hole. "Well, Papa, and William, I hope you rest in peace, if it is really you inside those coffins," she murmured, causing her grandfather to shake his head at her. What had she done wrong? Surely, she was allowed to talk to them?

A moment later her grandfather disappeared.

She hadn't used her handkerchief, so should she try to squeeze out a few tears? Her mother stood staring into the hole. At her sad face, real tears fell. Tears for her mother, more than for herself. She put her arm around her, but felt her stiffen and moan. "Mama, come away. It's all over."

"It's only just beginning," her mother said through gritted teeth.

"What do you mean?" She tried to turn her around to follow everybody else, but she remained fast, as if rooted to the spot. "Mama, come on."

"I can't. The baby—it's coming."

"No, Mama, Missus Edwards from next door didn't bring him. She thought it wouldn't be a good idea. If we need her later, she said she'll come round and help."

"Not that baby, this one."

Gasping with shock as, with a strangled cry, her mother gripped her belly, Harriet cast her eyes around for help.

Father Lane, their parish priest, came across and bent towards her, his hands clasped together. "Missus Harding. We need to go."

"I think she's having the baby," yelped Harriet. "Help her."

The priest's eyes opened wide and fear covered his face. "Baby? You mean...?"

Her grandfather reappeared. "I've found a midwife. I thought I recognised her in the crowd."

"How did you know, Gampy?" asked Harriet.

"That doesn't matter." He took her mother's arm. "Come on, my dear. We need to take you home speedily."

"But I can't walk. I daren't move in case it comes out. Oo, oo, help me."

The midwife put her hand on her stomach. "You want to push already?"

Her mother nodded.

"Dearie, dearie me." She looked around as if for inspiration. Several of the mourners had stopped to watch as the cart that had transported her father's coffin pulled away.

"Stop!" Harriet shouted. "Stop, we need you!"

The driver turned as she ran towards him. "Me, miss? But the funeral's over."

"I know that, but we need someone to take my mother home immediately. She's having a baby."

"What, now, this very minute?"

"Yes, help."

Her mother was steered towards them. As she lifted her foot to climb the step, she screamed, "Quick, it's coming."

The men looked the other way when the midwife lifted her skirts and immediately held up a tiny, wriggly baby. "It's a girl. You have a baby girl," she pronounced.

Harriet heard a mewling cry and then everyone cheered, the men still facing the other way, their innate sense of decorum taking over from their curiosity.

Not so her grandfather. He took off his coat and wrapped it around the baby. "God be praised," he shouted, holding her up. "One life ends and another begins."

"God be praised," repeated everyone else, this time looking at the gift from heaven.

Pulling down her skirts to hide her modesty, her mother raised her arms. "Let me see."

With tears in his eyes, Gampy handed the baby to her. "She has a look of her father around her eyes."

"So she does."

The midwife clicked her tongue. "We need you home, missus, so I can clean you up."

Her grandfather slipped the driver a coin as he climbed up and sat with his daughter. "Pray, sir, take us to Hare Street, if you would."

"Certainly, sir."

Harriet waved. "I'll catch you up."

"Well, it's not everybody who's born on a hearse cart," she heard her grandfather say as it pulled away. The clip-clopping of the horse's hooves prevented her from hearing her mother's reply.

"What a turn up for the books," exclaimed one of the mourners who had stayed to watch.

Harriet turned from watching the cart disappear out of sight to see Missus Bowe. "Yes, I didn't think the baby was due for a few weeks."

"Ah, the wonders of Nature. She can turn a tragedy into a triumph sometimes. I remember once…"

Harriet didn't want to hear the woman's story; she wanted to be left alone. Pretending to listen, by adding the occasional "Ah, yes" or "Oh, no", she accompanied her neighbour along the streets they had just walked. She didn't have an excuse not to go with her. Where else would she go?

"I suppose you'll be going to work, now?" Missus Bowe surprised her by asking.

"I hadn't really thought about it."

"Well, your grandfather won't be able to support you all, and your mother won't be fit for a few weeks. Our Lucy likes her job in the shop. Would you like me to ask her if they need anybody else?"

"I haven't finished school. My papa wouldn't have wanted me to leave yet."

"Well, he should have thought about that before he…"

Harriet stopped. "Before he what?"

Missus Bowe carried on walking and Harriet ran to catch her up. "Before he jumped off the bridge, do you mean?"

"I didn't mean anything. I should keep my big gob shut."

"Is that what everybody thinks? That he committed suicide? He wouldn't have, not my papa. Father Lane says suicide is a mortal sin. He'd go to Hell if he did something like that. And, anyway, Father Lane wouldn't have given him a proper burial if he had."

"You Catholics," scoffed Missus Bowe, stopping to look in a milliner's shop window. "Just look at that hat, would you? Isn't that the most adorable thing you've ever seen?"

Harriet glanced at the green hat with tulle around the brim. Just an ordinary hat to her. Without replying, she carried on alone. Surely her father hadn't killed himself? Wouldn't her ma have told her? But she wouldn't want her worrying about his soul, lost forever.

Staring up at the clouds, she tried to see him. Not taking notice of where she was walking, she bumped into a perambulator someone had left outside a shop, stubbing her toe on the wheel. "Ouch," she murmured. "Blinking perambulators, cluttering up the pavement." She felt like kicking it, but inside she could see a tiny baby's face, peeping up at her, the rest of its body well-wrapped against the cold. "It isn't your fault I'm in such a dudgeon," she told him.

With a huge sigh, she carried on walking. Missus Bowe had disappeared, probably gone into the milliners to try on the hat. She wouldn't be able to afford it, so what would be the point? But some people enjoyed looking at things they knew they'd have no possibility of buying. It made them feel better, gave them a diversion from their squalid lives for a fleeting moment.

Dragging her feet along the busy pavement, she took out her handkerchief and blew her nose. Why had they died? And would she have to leave school to find a job? Maybe she could work in the library? But her mathematical skills would stand her in better stead in a shop, for she could add up several numbers in her head. She stopped beside a bakery. Yes, that would be good. She'd be able to eat cakes, and even take a bun or two home to Gampy and Mama, if there were any left over at the end of the day.

Before her courage could desert her, she opened the door and went inside. A round woman with a kindly face stood behind the counter, and she waded straight in. "Please Missus, can I come and work for you?"

The lady's startled face stared at her for a moment, then she asked, "And who, pray, are you?"

"Harriet Harding, ma'am. My papa's just died and I need a job. I thought a bakery would be just right for me." She sniffed the wonderful aroma of fresh bread. "Um, delicious."

"And you thought you'd be able to eat cake all day, did you?" asked the baker.

"No, ma'am, certainly not." Not all day, anyway, but how had she guessed? Harriet looked longingly at the array of pastries and fancy cakes on the counter.

"Well, I don't need nobody, so clear off."

The woman didn't need to be so rude, and so much for the kindly-looking face. "Well, I wouldn't want to work for someone as horrid as you, anyway." She ran out, tempted to grab a cake but her conscience stopped her in time and, anyway, she didn't want the woman coming after her brandishing a rolling pin.

What next? The ironmongers didn't appeal, nor did the blacksmith on the corner. *Don't be silly,* she told herself. *As if he'd employ a girl.* The haberdashery shop; that was a different matter. She could see herself measuring out pretty ribbons, blue and green and pink.

"Would that satisfy madam?" she rehearsed putting on a high-class voice. It didn't quite succeed, but with practice it might come. She had only ever been inside such a shop once, and the array of materials and lace and buttons had thrilled her.

She patted down her skirt and, tucking her curly hair into her bonnet, opened the door, a broad smile on her lips, thinking she would look more presentable with a happy face rather than a stern or sad one.

Don't go marching in like last time, she told herself, ambling over to pretend an interest in a tartan cloth.

The shopkeeper finished serving her customer and came across. "May I help you?" She stood in front of the material, as if guarding it.

Straightening her back and tilting her head to one side, Harriet asked, in as refined a voice as she could, "Good day, ma'am, are you the proprietor of this fair establishment?" *That should impress her.*

"And what if I am?"

"I was wondering, ma'am," she made a sweeping arc with her hand, "Seeing as this is such a beautiful shop…"

The shopkeeper looked her up and down, clearly unimpressed. "Stop wasting my time, and skedaddle."

"But, ma'am, I was wondering if you needed an assistant," she gushed as the woman walked to the counter.

That stopped her.

"You see, my father has just passed away, ma'am, and my mother and me…" That didn't sound right. Should it be me or I? Just carry on. "My mother has had a baby and I need a job to support them." No need to mention Gampy. He might go off to sea again.

The woman had reached the counter and she turned and looked Harriet over once more. "What recommendations do you have?"

"I can sew. My ma says as how I am the best needlewoman she has ever seen." A big exaggeration, but not an actual lie.

"And?"

"And, and…I can knit."

The woman grunted.

"I can add up ever so fast. Please, miss…um, ma'am…"

The doorbell pinged and two ladies came in, chattering and giggling. "Oo, look, Loretta, do you not think that blue silk would match my eyes?" One of them stroked a swathe of royal blue material.

"My, my, Maria, it would be perfect."

The door opened again and more customers entered. One of them dropped a handkerchief, and Harriet rushed to pick it up. The lady thanked her without looking at her and continued examining a tray of buttons.

Watching as they were served, keeping out of the way, but taking note of the prices, she added them up in her head as the shopkeeper wrapped them in an envelope of white paper.

"Sixpence," she whispered.

The shopkeeper glanced over and nodded. Once the ladies had all been served, she turned to Harriet. "I could certainly do with an extra pair of hands, but…" She looked Harriet up and down again. "You will need to wear something a little more…how shall I put it?"

Harriet's heart sank. She hadn't thought about her clothes. She didn't own anything suitable, and had no money to buy anything.

The shopkeeper must have realised her quandary. "I tell you what. I have a dress that does not fit me any more." She patted her midriff. "I have put on weight since I married my good husband. He insists on me eating too much. But never mind that. You look like a trustworthy sort of gal. Come back at five o'clock and I shall find it for you. If it fits, you may start work tomorrow."

"Thank you, thank you, ma'am. My mama will be so pleased."

She rushed out, forgetting to ask the lady's name, so ran back in. "I'm sorry, ma'am, but I don't know your name,"

"Miss Louisa Little."

"But I thought you said you were married."

"I am, but I keep my professional life separate from my personal one."

Harriet stared at her in amazement. "I thought all women took their husband's name when they married."

"I did. My married name is Lighten, but I prefer to use my maiden name. Anyway, you have not told me yours. I cannot employ someone without a name." Missus Lighten's or Little's eyes twinkled, putting Harriet at her ease. The lady looked rather old to be recently married, though, at least thirty.

"Miss Harriet Harding at your service, Miss Little." She gave a curtsy, bringing a smile to her new employer's face.

"Harding? My mother's maiden name was Harding. I wonder if we could be related."

"I doubt it, ma'am."

"Which part of London does your father hail from?"

Not ashamed of her roots, but not wanting to admit where she lived, she wondered how to reply. A customer came in, so she was spared. "See you later," she called as she went out. The lady would find out eventually as she'd need her address. Make one up? But she might need to contact her.

The rest of the way home she skipped along as if her feet were on wheels, even when she passed groups of filthy children, sitting on the steps of the larger, run-down houses. This must be what it's like to ride one of those bicycles things, she thought. Maybe I'll earn enough money to buy one, and then I won't have to walk everywhere. Crossing the road, to cut off the corner, she was nearly knocked down by one, ridden by a young lady who wobbled precariously, probably on her first outing. *I'd have to learn to ride better than that,* she grinned.

On arrival, she flung open the door, calling, "Mama, Gampy, you'll never guess what I've done."

"Shush, child. Do you have to be so loud?" her grandfather called from the kitchen. "Your mother's trying to rest."

"I'm sorry, Gampy. I was excited…" Her jaw dropped as she looked at what he held. Two tiny babies. "That isn't Tommy. Where did the other one come from?"

"He was born on the way home."

"What do you mean?"

Gampy shook his head. "I mean, child, that on our way home your mother produced a second baby."

"What? On the cart?"

"Yes." He nodded, handing one of them to her. "So we have two new mouths to feed."

"Three, if Missus Edwards next door don't keep Tommy."

"Hopefully she will. She came round earlier and asked to look after him another night."

She peered into the sleeping baby's face. "Is it a boy or a girl?"

"I can't tell them apart yet. All babies look the same to me." Studying them both, he added, "I think that's the girl."

"So the newest one is a boy?"

"Yes, twin boy and girl. I hope these two survive, not like the other twins, Doris and Edmund. They didn't live a week."

"I don't remember them. They were born when I was a little girl, weren't they?" At his nod, she continued, "Is Mama going to call them by the same names?"

"I haven't asked her yet. I'd have thought she'd want to call the boy Thomas, after your father."

"But we already have Tommy."

"I know, but, strictly, he isn't ours. Anyway, what were you so excited about when you came in?"

Her news had lost its sparkle. But her wage would be needed even more, so it should be twice as important. "I found a job."

"You found a job? Who for? Your mother won't be in a position to…"

"For me, Gampy, for me."

"What are you talking about, child?"

"Well, I thought, and Missus Bowe hinted, that I'd need to work, seeing as we won't have Papa's wages, so I went into a shop and asked if I could work there, and the lady a lovely lady called Miss Little, although she isn't really a miss she's a missus, well, she said I can start tomorrow."

"Slow down, child. I can hardly understand you."

She took a deep breath. "It's true, Gampy. I have to go back at five o'clock today and she says she'll give me, or did she say lend? I don't remember. Anyway, she has a dress that doesn't fit her anymore because she's put weight on, so she says, but I thought she looked rather fine."

Her grandfather pulled a face, took the baby into the front room, laid it in a wooden drawer, already decked out with blankets, and she carried in the other baby. "Where shall I put this one?"

He placed it next to its twin, frowning.

"Aren't you pleased for me, Gampy? Don't you think I done well?"

"Did well, child, not done."

She tugged at his sleeve as he turned to walk to the kitchen. "Gampy?"

He poured water out of the kettle into the teapot. "Cuppa?"

She'd thought he'd be over the moon that she'd used her initiative, and couldn't understand his attitude. "Yes, please. Shall I take one up to Mama? She'll be pleased at my news, even if you're not."

"It isn't that I'm displeased." He swallowed hard before continuing, "I want to be the breadwinner. Your father didn't want you to leave school before you took your exams."

"I know, Gampy, but what is it you always say? Needs must when the devil drives? And he seems to have driven a long way, or is it a hard bargain? Whatever it is, I thought I was doing the right thing." With a heavy heart, she picked up a cup and saucer to take upstairs.

Her mother asleep, she put the cup down carefully on the bedside table, so as not to wake her. But she needed to give her the news, to see her reaction. Her face looked peaceful in sleep. She couldn't disturb her. Coping with two babies would take all her energy. She wondered why the other twins had died. After her brother and father, she prayed these two would not.

Neighbours arrived for the wake and she hoped they wouldn't wake her mother as they made a fuss of the twins, all talking at once.

Chapter 12

Harriet doubted she'd done the right thing. Her grandfather had barely spoken to her since she'd told him her news. She took the babies upstairs to her mother to be fed and the one who had to wait cried so much it gave her a headache. Her mother too busy to listen to her, she went out to walk the mile or so to the haberdashery shop.

As she passed the Leekes' house, Missus Leekes came out, holding Isabel by the hand. "My dear, how are you faring?" she asked, patting Harriet's arm. "It was so sad, what happened."

Isabel put her arms around her legs. "I sorry, too."

As much as she had not felt like crying at the burial, tears filled her eyes at their compassion. She brushed them off with her gloved hand, noticing the holes in the fingertips. "I...I'm faring quite well, thank you."

"And your mother?"

"She's had twins." Harriet stared at the gloves. If she worked hard she might be able to buy herself a pair of new ones.

"I beg your pardon."

"My mother gave birth to twins, just after the funeral."

Missus Leekes put her hand to her mouth. "I thought that was what you said. But...but the funeral was only a few hours ago. I'm so sorry I couldn't make it, but young John was restless, and there was nobody to leave him with."

"Don't vex yourself, Missus Leekes," Harriet surprised herself by replying. She would need to start using more grown-up phrases now she was a working girl. "But I must dash." She couldn't afford to be late. Miss Little might change her mind.

"Give your mother my regards and tell her I'll pop round in the morning to see if she needs anything."

"Thank you. I will. Good day." She hurried away before the lady could detain her any longer. She meant well, but Harriet had neither the time nor the inclination to stand chatting.

The shop door opened as she stood staring at it, afraid to go in. What if Miss Little had decided she did not need an assistant after all? What if the dress she'd said she could have didn't fit? So many what ifs.

The two ladies, who had been in the shop earlier, the ones examining the blue silk, came out with a brown parcel.

"I had to come back for it. I knew it would be perfect," the one called Loretta said to the other one, pushing past Harriet as if she were not there. Could she be polite to ladies like that? Bite her tongue if they were rude to her? But why would they be? If she were standing behind a counter, she'd be a person they'd notice, not a nobody in a tatty black dress. Black dress! What if the one Miss Little was about to give her was bright pink or shocking yellow? How would she wear that at home, when everybody else would be dressed in black?

Five minutes later she still stood there, watching people come and go, wanting to enter, but afraid there would be too many problems. Finally, Miss Little herself came out, dressed in her outdoor clothes. It had to be now or never, or she'd miss her chance. She rushed up to her as she turned the key in the lock.

"Miss Little, am I too late? Please say I am not. I'm sorry I was not here at five o'clock, although actually I was but…"

"Ah, Harriet, I thought you had changed your mind."

"No, Miss Little." She bit her lip, praying her boat had not sailed, or whatever the expression was.

Miss Little opened the door and lit a lamp. "You had better come in."

"Thank you, thank you. My ma's had twins, you know. She had another one on the way home."

"Today?"

"Yes, so I need a job more than ever."

Miss Little's brow furrowed, or maybe the light from the lamp made it look like it was as she surveyed Harriet. "I shall fetch the dress. You wait here. No, on second thoughts, come with me. I…I would not want to leave you in the dark."

Harriet knew she'd been wary about trusting her not to steal something, but she fully understood. The lady couldn't know what an honest person she was, and there were so many rough characters about, she had cause for concern about leaving an unknown girl in a shop full of valuable silks and things.

Upstairs, they waded through piles of materials and boxes. "I used to live here, would you believe?" Miss Little said as they entered one of the rooms and made enough space to open a wardrobe door, revealing a rack full of dresses of every colour. "Which one would you like?"

Harriet ran her fingers along them. "My goodness, Miss Little, don't any of them fit you anymore?"

"I am ashamed to say not." She took out a pretty pink one and held it against Harriet. "This one would suit you."

"It's a little too…um, I mean. It's beautiful, but…" How could she voice her needs without offending the lady? "You see, we're in mourning…"

"Of course, silly me, you need black or purple. Well, fear not, young maiden, I have just the one." She took out a dark-coloured bustle dress.

"It's…um…it's…"

"Too old-fashioned, isn't it? You're right. We don't wear bustles any more. Let me see what else I have."

Harriet could not believe how many dresses she owned. And none of them fitted. Why did she not sell them?

"What about this? I could alter it if need be; it would not take me long."

The purple velvet dress looked ideal, with a high-necked collar and pleated ruffles. But how could she wear such a garment?

"Would you like to try it on?"

"Now?"

"I won't know if it fits if you don't. I shall not look, if it's your modesty you're worried about."

It wasn't her modesty but her holey vest, and her petticoat that wasn't much better.

"Are you sure you have the time? I mean, it takes me a while to undo all the laces and buttons."

"I shall help. Come here."

There was nothing for it but to comply. Ten minutes later, having managed not to let the lady see her old underwear, she stood looking in the mirror at a different person. Could it really be her, Harriet Harding, staring back at her?

"I always wanted curls like yours," remarked her new employer, picking one up and twisting it in her fingers. "But my hair just hangs lank and straight. That's why I put it in a bun. It doesn't matter, then, how straight or lank it is."

"Sometimes curls can be a disadvantage. At school, they're always telling me to tuck them in."

"Well, I shall not. I shall allow them to hang down your back, with the merest little scarf to keep them off your face. What do you think about the dress? It looks very becoming, in my opinion."

"Yes, it does. It's too grand for me."

"Fie, how can you say that? And it does not need altering at all. I knew it would fit you perfectly. I have an eye for such matters." She helped her undo the little buttons and Harriet quickly donned her old dress.

"I expect you are wondering why I keep them?" Miss Little surprised her by saying. "Well, my husband only wants me to wear clothes he buys me. These belong to my old life, the life I led before he came on the scene. I keep

82

them for emotional reasons. Silly, I know, but I take them out and look at them now and again. Not that I am unhappy with him. Don't get me wrong. I am. I had begun to think I had been left on the shelf until he came along. He is a little older than me, actually, a lot older; almost in his dotage."

"And how old is that?" Harriet had the temerity to ask. It might be construed as being impertinent, but the lady made her at ease, and she found herself saying things she wouldn't normally say.

"Sixty-eight."

Harriet gasped. "That's older than my grandfather, and he's that old I sometimes worry he'll die."

"Well, yes, I have that concern occasionally, especially when I see him sitting in his chair with his eyes closed. But I do not worry for long. I shall be a very wealthy lady when he does…you know, leave this mortal coil."

"And are you expecting that to be soon?"

"Oh, no, no, no, not at all. Do not get me wrong. I love him dearly."

"I feel a 'but' coming."

Miss Little laughed, a tinkly sound that reminded Harriet of the bell above the door downstairs. She tugged Harriet's sleeve. "Come on, your mother will be wondering where you have gone." She turned as they reached the door. "Are you taking the dress now, or changing into it on your arrival in the morning?"

Tempted to say she would take it, but fearful that something might happen to it on her way home, or the following day—even though pickpockets would not be able to magic it away from her arms—she said she would change in the morning.

Miss Little locked the shop once more and, wrapping her shawl around her, bade Harriet a fond farewell and hurried off in the opposite direction to the one Harriet would take.

Harriet stood looking in the window, not that she could see much in the dim light from the lamppost further along the street. She couldn't make out any prices, so imagined what they would be and practised adding them up in her head.

Chapter 13

Her face ruddy from the cold, Harriet thought she heard her mother talking as she went upstairs. "Who are you speaking to, Mama? It can't be the babies, for they're asleep."

"Your father, dearie. It seems he's still here in the room with me." Harriet's gaze followed hers as she glanced up at the spot, but a look of horror came over her face.

"What's the matter, dear?" her mother asked. "I didn't mean he's really there."

She glanced away, afraid to see her dead father somehow reappear. "No, Mama, it's just that...no...nothing."

"Have you been out?" She moved her leg and patted a spot on the bed for Harriet to sit down. "You look cold."

"Yes, Mama, I've saved us from ig...ignominy."

"That's rather a grand word, dearie, but tell me, how have you done this great deed?"

"I've found myself a position as a haberdashery assistant."

Her mother blinked hard. "A haberdashery assistant, eh? Well, well, I always knew you were a reliant sort of girl. But when did this happen?"

"While you were giving birth to my new baby brother, apparently. Gampy told me he had to help deliver him."

She laughed. "Yes, your poor grandfather. I don't know who was more embarrassed."

Harriet leaned over and stroked one of them on the cheek. "Which is which?"

Her mother pointed to the boy. "He's slightly bigger."

"What's his name?"

"I haven't decided yet." Shaking her head, she pouted. "That was what I was talking to your father about. He wants the same as the other little angels we lost, but I'm not sure."

"Me neither. We need something cheerful, like…" Harriet puffed out her cheeks. "Um…how about Rebecca and Ralph?"

"Um, Rebecca, perhaps, but not Ralph. I knew a man called that, when I was a little girl, and he…well, let's say I don't want to be reminded of him each time I see my little boy."

"Well, how about William?" suggested Harriet after a moment. "After Gampy and William Henry?"

"Now that I could live with. William it is, William Thomas."

Harriet jumped up. "I'll give Gampy the good news. Maybe he won't be so out of sorts with me for finding the job."

"Why on earth would your grandfather be out of sorts when you've used your initiative and saved us from…what was the word you used"

"Igmoniny. No, that's not it. I remembered it first time, but can't say it now," Harriet giggled. "And that's what I told him, but he thinks he won't be needed if I can earn a crust."

"Piffle, as if we'd think that."

Gampy came in with a plate of hot soup. "You rang, milady?"

"Ah, that smells nice. Have you made it yourself?"

"Yes, with my own fair rubber bands. I hope it is to your satisfaction."

"I'm sure it will be." Her mother took a sip. It burned her lip. "Ouch, it's hot."

"Well, you'd complain if it were cold."

Another sip proved less hurtful when she blew it first. "Umm, this is delicious. I didn't know you were so skilful."

"There's a lot you don't know about me."

She pointed to Harriet. "Hasn't she done well, finding a job at her first attempt?"

"Well, I think she should remain at school, at least until she's finished her exams. You know that's what her father wanted."

"Papa, if she'd been a boy, I'd readily agree with you, but she's only a girl, so education isn't important. Look at me. I left school at thirteen, even younger than she is. It didn't do me any harm, did it?"

"Well, only because you met your Thomas and married him as soon as you were old enough."

"True, but I had been working, even though it wasn't well-paid. You were always away at sea, and when Mama became ill, she needed my wage. My little brothers, Joe and Fred, didn't earn much, crawling under the machines to keep them working."

"I had to earn my crust somehow." He wrung his hands, "And the sea had beckoned me since I was a little boy. I ran away to join a ship when I was but twelve years old." He stood up straight, sticking out his chest. "But I never regretted it."

Harriet sat listening to them, not wanting to interrupt.

Finishing off her soup, her mother handed him the empty plate. "I'm not criticising you, Papa. There's no need to go all defensive. I'm just saying."

"Well, what's done is done. We can't turn back the clock, not that I would want to. I had a good life at sea and enjoyed every minute of it."

"And told Harriet some whopping stories, most of them made up, I'm sure."

Harriet grinned. "Really, Mama?"

He laughed as he went towards the door. "Maybe inflated slightly, but most of them true. I'll leave you to rest now, my dear daughter, before the next assault."

Harriet also stood up but hesitated. "How did you meet Papa?"

"I caught his eye across the floor of the factory where I worked. Even at fifteen, I was buxom, and he told me, after we were married, that it was my figure that first attracted him. Cheeky beggar. It was his big brown eyes that I noticed. They melted my heart. Not that we spoke for weeks, just mooned over each other from a distance, until that fateful day, when one of the children caught his sleeve in my machine and his arm was yanked off at the shoulder, right under me. Thomas raced over to disentangle the boy, and I plucked up the courage to speak to him, once the child was carted away. From that moment onwards, I was smitten. We met after work and talked and talked, and walked and walked, anywhere, just happy to be together."

One of the babies stirred, so she undid the laces on her nightgown and Harriet took her cue to leave.

Chapter 14

Hardly sleeping a wink all night, in case she overslept, Harriet left the house in plenty of time, wishing she had timed how long it had taken from her house to the shop the previous evening. She did not own a watch, so how could she have done?

She raced along the streets, scared she would be late on her first day, but the CLOSED sign on the shop door told her she had arrived before her employer. A few deep breaths, and she felt prepared for a hard day's work. Being Saturday, she knew it would be busy.

Taking a closer look at the items in the window, she laughed. They were not at all what she had imagined the previous evening. A roll of red ribbon and a skein of red embroidery silk had been placed in such a way that they resembled a heart. It would not be Saint Valentine's day for another two months. Christmas was just around the corner. Baubles and silvery items would be more appropriate. Maybe her first job might be brightening up the window display to attract more customers. Miss Little had clearly not done anything with it for months, for a cobweb dangled from a roll of material to a card of ribbon.

Although sweat had been running down her back from the hurried walk, she shivered, hoping Miss Little wouldn't be much longer. Raindrops started to fall and she sheltered in the shop doorway as the street became busy with passers-by.

A nearby clock struck the hour and on the count of nine—she always counted things like that, a sometimes irritating habit—the lady appeared, out of breath. "Ah, Harriet," she gasped. "I hope I have not kept you waiting too long."

"No, no, Miss Little." She tried not to show how cold she was as they hurried inside and Miss Little lit a lamp. Although it was daylight, the cloudy skies made the interior of the shop gloomy.

The door bell pinged before they had removed their coats, and a refined lady walked in.

"Good day, madam," offered Miss Little. "Pray excuse me a moment. Would madam like to browse for a few minutes while I…?"

The customer didn't give her time to finish. "I would like those grey gloves in your window, if you please."

"Yes, ma'am, certainly, ma'am." Wriggling back into her coat, Miss Little hurried over to the window and picked up the gloves.

"You see, the stitching has come loose on these." The lady took off one she was wearing as the bell tinkled once more.

A young girl ran in. "Mama, why did you not wait for me?"

"You should keep up," replied her mother, not looking at the girl, but handing the faulty glove to Miss Little.

Miss Little examined it. "You did not buy these here."

"Did I say I did? No, I am just showing you."

A look of relief came over Miss Little's face as she wrapped up the new pair.

Harriet watched the interaction, wondering if she should do something. But what? The girl glanced at her. Did she look out of place? Should she tidy up the array of embroidery silks or would the girl think she was trying to steal them? In her old, shabby dress, they would never imagine her to be the new assistant. To put them straight, she asked, "Miss Little, shall I go through to the back and…you know?" She gestured to her dress.

"Yes, yes, off you go."

Running through the shop and upstairs, Harriet yanked off her dress, replacing it with the new second-hand one, smiling to herself. How could a second-hand article be new?

Miss Little hadn't said she'd ever had a maid, but how else would she fasten all the buttons down the back of the dress? One of Harriet's friends had gone into service in a big house, miles away in the country and, on one of her afternoons off, had told her about maids and servants. But she didn't have time to daydream, so she hurried down to find the glove lady had gone.

"She was a tartar, wasn't she?" she remarked.

"Who?" Miss Little looked up from the notebook she'd been studying.

"The glove lady."

"That's nothing compared to some people who come in here. Come here and let me do you up. You have the wrong buttons in the wrong buttonholes."

Thankful she'd taken extra care having a wash, even though she hadn't had time to heat the water for a bath, she prayed that running half the way there didn't make her smell. It would have been embarrassing to have such a fine lady touch her if she smelled of sweat. However, Miss Little didn't turn up her nose or make any remark.

The dress duly fastened to her satisfaction, Miss Little returned to her book. "I have been thinking of a way to save money. With so much stock, I shall have a sale after Christmas, when everybody is pulling in the purse strings and wanting to save a penny here and there."

"But surely reducing prices will bring in less money?"

"Ah, but I can sell off items that don't sell at the full price, thus raising extra revenue that I would not normally make, if that makes sense."

Harriet considered the proposal. "Yes, I see what you mean. What shall I do? I don't know what sells well and what doesn't. But I thought, looking in the window this morning, that I might clear it out and make a Christmas display."

"A fine idea. Yes, start right away. I have rather neglected it of late and a Christmas display would cheer us all. How about a cup of tea first?"

"That would be lovely, thank… Oh, you want me to make it?" Harriet had been looking forward to getting stuck in, but realised her duties would be menial to start with.

Having lit the fire and set the kettle to boil, she left cups and teapot ready and went through to the shop. Several customers had come in, and she wondered if she'd be allowed to serve. Miss Little hadn't informed her of her duties. But she didn't know the prices.

About to make a start on the window, she tried not to panic when a customer asked to see tapestry wools, and Miss Little was busy serving another lady. Um, wools? She could see blank tapestry cloths hanging up, but no wool. Maybe in one of the drawers? After opening several, and unable to find any, she had nothing for it but to ask.

"I'm sorry to keep you, ma'am, but it's my first day," she whispered to the lady who stood patiently waiting. "I shall locate them for you straightaway."

She lingered until Miss Little had finished speaking and asked in a soft voice, "Tapestry wools?"

The shopkeeper pointed to another set of drawers covered in packages, and Harriet turned back to her customer. "Here they are, ma'am." She tried to speak in a refined manner. "What colour are you looking for?"

"Um…" the lady picked up a blue one. "No, this is not the right shade."

"How about this one?" asked Harriet, picking out a lighter one.

"Too light."

"Or this one?"

"Too dark."

Taking a deep breath, and fixing a smile to her mouth, she showed her every blue wool in the drawer.

"I think I shall leave it," said the lady, tying her bonnet ribbons. "Maybe the shop up the road will have the exact colour I want." And she went out, leaving Harriet feeling she had failed in her first attempt at serving. She wouldn't be kept on if she couldn't sell something small.

"I'm so sorry," she moaned to Miss Little a minute later, when the shop emptied. "I couldn't even sell a skein of wool."

"Do not worry about it, my dear. We cannot satisfy everybody."

"But I need to earn my wages."

"You carry on with the window and let me worry about everything else. Later, we can go over prices and that sort of thing."

"Thank you, Miss Little. I'll make the tea first."

"Good girl, and why don't you call me Miss Louisa. Not in front of customers, but on our own it would be fine."

"I'm not sure if I should. Wouldn't it be impolite?"

"Not at all."

Pouring out the tea, she couldn't believe her luck, landing such a job with such an friendly employer.

Several hours later, her stomach rumbled. Being nervous, she hadn't eaten breakfast, and hadn't considered lunch. At home, they often forwent a meal in the middle of the day, depending on finances, so it hadn't occurred to her to bring anything. What would her employer do? She hadn't had chance to call her by her Christian name, and kept practising it in her head. Louisa was an attractive name and she sometimes wished she had a prettier one, but Harriet was better than some.

Despite the rain, she went outside to take a look at her display. "Very striking, even though I say it myself," she muttered. Hurrying back inside, she collided with a tall gentleman, walking with a cane, whom she had expected to carry on along the street, not to go into the shop.

"I beg your pardon, young lady," he said, bowing as he held the door open for her.

"Sorry, sir," she replied, ducking under his arm.

"Lancelot!" exclaimed Miss Louisa, turning to see the latest invader. "I had not expected to see you today."

He glanced over at Harriet. "I came to make sure everything was in order."

What did he mean? Had he assumed, because she was not a rich girl, that she would be delving into the till or pocketing the wares while her employer's back was turned? She felt like turning out her pockets to show him, but she did not have any, of course, not in her new dress.

"Why would it not be?" asked Miss Louisa. She evidently trusted her. "It is very 'in order'. Did you not see the magnificent window display Harriet has put together? And we have been busier than usual. The word has probably gone the rounds that I have a new assistant and everybody is coming in to take a gander at her, not that I'm complaining, if they buy something while they're having a butchers."

Harriet had not noticed people taking a gander at her. She had been too busy deciding how to arrange the baubles and paper chains Miss Louisa had ferreted out from a cupboard in the back room.

"Please do not use such common words, my dear." The man took off his hat and placed it on the counter, showering droplets of rain onto her book.

"Please, dear…" she began but, with one look from him, she stopped. "Anyway, may I introduce my new…assistant and friend, Harriet? Harriet, this is my husband, Mister Lighten."

Harriet stepped forward, wondering whether to curtsy. Taking in his white hair and thin lips, she bobbed a small one, just in case. He was not at all as she had expected. Thin lips were a sign of meanness, her grandfather told her. Miss Louisa had insinuated that her husband was a generous man, but from first impressions, she found him to be a bossy one.

"She appears very young."

"I am nearly fourteen, sir, and…"

The forbidding raising of his eyebrows told her to stop. He'd probably say she should only speak when spoken to, that she should wait for his approval.

"But she is very willing," cut in Miss Louisa, in her defence. She removed his hat from the counter and put it behind her as three elderly ladies came in.

Mister Lighten reached out for it. "I am not staying, my dear. I wish you farewell." He grabbed the hat and went out without giving Harriet another glance.

Pretending to finish her display, Harriet waited until the ladies had been served and went over to Miss Louisa. "Your husband was not as I had pictured him."

"No, probably not. I try to describe him in a favourable light, as a dutiful wife should, but…" She fiddled with the end of the roll from the lady's order. "I had thought to ask him if he would take us for a bite to eat, but seeing as he did not seem in a pleasant mood, I decided not to."

Thank goodness, thought Harriet. *I wouldn't have been easy, eating whilst he watched my every move.* "Does he come into the shop often?" she asked instead.

"No, no, very rarely. He…" She cleared her throat. "He keeps himself busy in other ways, thank God. He would want to interfere with how I run it. I know him. He would not be able to help himself, so it is much easier if he stays away."

"Yes, I suppose it would be difficult to run it in your own way with him breathing down your neck." Harriet felt bold to have spoken in such a familiar manner, but Miss Louisa didn't seem to notice as she went through to the back. "Put your coat on, my dear. We are closing for dinner."

Should she admit she had no money?

"It will be my treat, to thank you for being so artistic and brightening my window." After turning the OPEN sign to CLOSED, she locked the door and surveyed the colourful display. "This should bring in more customers." She peered closer. "Ah, is that a little lamb, next to the angel? How sweet. I love lambs. Not that I see any. If only we lived in the countryside. We should be able to see them everyday—in the spring, of course. They soon grow into sheep, so I am told. They don't remain little, frolicking lovelies for long."

Harriet had never seen one, except in books, and did not know how sweet they were. It had seemed a good idea to put the furry animal next to the angels. After all, the Bible told that the shepherds brought them to the stable where the baby Jesus was born. But if they were only lambs in the spring, how come they were there when Jesus was born in the winter? She had no chance to ask, for Miss Louisa had moved onto a different subject until they arrived at the teashop.

The rest of the day passed quickly, with Harriet tidying up the interior of the shop, with rolls of silk and taffeta sorted into colours, starting from the palest to the darkest, and the drawers in the same way. By closing time she had rearranged practically everything, to the extent that Miss Louisa complained she would be unable to find anything, having been used to the muddle for so long. But she admitted how much more organised it looked, and praised Harriet for her fine work.

"Tomorrow, or rather on Monday for, of course we do not open on a Sunday, now you have organised my stock, I might ask you to start on the storeroom," she declared before she waved goodbye.

Harriet had been anticipating that, but her heart sank. She had looked in at one point in the afternoon, to find some red buttons Miss Louisa had sworn would be in there, but had not been able to find them amongst the piles of unsorted wares.

"Have you had a good day?" asked her grandfather on her arrival home.

"Oh, yes, Gampy." She told him all about it.

"Well, it beats working in a factory, I suppose, although…"

"Gampy, please do not start on about school again. Miss Louisa said I can have half an hour off on Monday to tell them I won't be returning."

He shrugged. "It's your choice, girl. I won't say I approve, but I'm proud of what you've done."

Hugging him, she asked what was for dinner.

"Shirt and tie, or should I say shepherd's pie, so you don't confuse it with anything else, made by my own fair brass bands. Can't you Aunt Nell it?"

"My darling Gampy, I'll never get used to your language, but yes, it smells delicious," she laughed. "How's Mama? May I go up and see her?"

"I think she's feeding one of the babies, so yes, off you go."

She entered her mother's bedroom and warmed her cold hands at the roaring fire.

"That's William done," her mother said as she held out the baby towards her. "The girl's still asleep, so I'll leave her. I can see no point in waking a slumbering baby."

Harriet took him and studied his face. She could see a definite likeness to her father. "Hello, William Thomas. How are you today?"

He burped as she lifted him onto her shoulder. "Good boy. That was better out than in."

Her mother patted the usual space at her side for Harriet to sit down. "How was your first day as an adult?"

"I never thought of it like that. It was good, actually." She told her all the events she could think of.

"Your Miss Louisa sounds a really nice person," answered her mother when she had finished. "I hope she keeps you on when you've finished reorganising her establishment."

"Mama, do you think she only wanted me for that long? I hadn't considered that. Maybe I should untidy it again on Monday, so I can retidy it on Tuesday, and do that every alternate day?"

Her mother laughed. "No, dearie, I don't think that at all."

"Anyway, by the state of the storeroom it'll probably take me a week, and I haven't learned any prices yet."

Chapter 15

Sunday being a day of rest, Harriet would normally have slept later but, because she shared with her mother, the babies woke her early.

"I wish I could help you feed them," she wailed, sitting up and rocking one of the twins.

"I might have to call on the services of Missus Leekes for this lusty little boy. Is she still feeding baby Tommy?"

"I suppose so. I feel guilty that I haven't been to see Missus Edwards from next door to check on him. Would she have enough milk to feed three babies, though?"

"Probably not. I'll have to manage. My milk should be through today. It takes a day or two."

"Mama?" Would it be a good time to ask her question again?

"Um?"

"You still haven't told me how the babies got in your tummy."

Her mother sighed. "It is really not the best... Very well. I suppose you need to know. Have your fairies arrived yet?"

"I don't think so."

"You'd know if they have. Have you had stomach aches?"

She shook her head.

"Well, you see, every month the mother has an egg inside her..."

The baby took that moment to vomit down Harriet's nightshirt. "Ugh, Ma!"

"Dear, oh, dear. She didn't take very much, and now she's brought it up. She'll never thrive at this rate." Her mother took the baby from her.

"But what about my nightshirt?"

"Your grandfather said he'll do the washing tomorrow, although I'm sure he doesn't know one end of a washtub from the other."

Harriet pulled the sicky garment over her head and, shivering, quickly dressed in her Sunday clothes. The dress was frayed at the edge of the high collar, but she could disguise it with a scarf. "I should have lit your fire first, before I put this on," she declared. "I hope I don't get coal dust on it."

"My apron's over there."

Having lit the fire and ensured her mother had everything she needed, she went downstairs to light the one in the lounge and boil the kettle, still none the wiser as to how babies were made.

Surprised her grandfather had not already risen, she made porridge and took some up to her mother with a cup of tea. "Gampy isn't up yet, Mama. He's usually the first to rise."

"Well, it is only six o'clock."

"Is it? Why on earth have I got up, then? I didn't think to look at the clock." She yawned. "Shall I come back to bed?"

"No, dearie, you're dressed now."

"I wondered why it was so dark."

Her mother laughed as she sipped her tea. But then she grew sober. "You will remember to say a prayer for your father and brother, won't you, when you go to Mass?"

She took a quick peek up at the corner, but the light from the candle flickered shadows anyway, so she could not be sure if she could see anything untoward. "Yes, of course. Do you think Gampy will go?"

"I don't know. You'll have to ask him when he arises. He does sometimes attend, or used to, when he came home on leave, but..." She shook her head and handed back the tray. "If you don't mind, I'll have a few hours sleep now the babies are settled."

"Yes, Mama." Harriet went out, wondering what she could do at such an unearthly hour of the morning. Maybe do some sums in case Miss Louisa wanted help with the books she always seemed to peruse.

Two hours later, she was awoken by her grandfather burping as he came into the lounge.

"You're up early," he said as he scratched his back and yawned.

She stretched and yawned. "I've been up ages. Are you coming to church?"

"Yes, yes, we need to pray for your father and brother, don't we?"

"Good." It comforted her that she wouldn't have to face everybody on her own. Normally, she would have attended with both her parents, but her father would never go again, and her mother not for a few weeks. Their friends and neighbours would be giving their best wishes and condolences. She knew from past experience when someone died that they would all gather round the bereaved as they filed out of the church. She couldn't face that on her own.

"Am I allowed anything to eat?" he asked as he put the kettle on to boil again.

"No, Gampy, not after midnight if you want to receive Holy Communion."

"But aren't I exempt for being an old pot and pan?"

She laughed. "You're not old."

"Well, I feel it this morning." He stretched, reaching his arms up to almost touch the ceiling.

"You shouldn't really even have tea, only water."

"I'll have it black. It'll only be water, then." With a lot of puffing and blowing, he sat down and his nightcap fell off.

Harriet bent to pick it up.

"Thank you. See if your mother's awake and take her a cup of rosie lee."

101

She had been about to say she had already had one, but that had been hours ago. She would probably welcome another. If only she, herself, could have one! "It will taste all the better for the wait," she could hear her father saying. *Papa, Papa, why did you have to die?*

An hour later, sitting in the large old church, listening to the sermon, it seemed as if the priest kept looking in her direction when he preached about forgiveness and reconciliation. How people should never go to bed on an argument. But she hadn't argued with her father. She tried to remember her last words to him. He had been rather curt, she recalled, but that hadn't been her fault. Should she have apologised before he left?

She came out of church more wretched and guilty than when she had gone in. There had not even been chance to look around for the boy who sometimes gave her a smile. She didn't know his name or his family, but looked forward to Sundays. Her heart gave a little flutter each time he looked at her with that smile.

Father Lane stood at the door, nodding to everyone, and he took the time to give his condolences once more to her and her grandfather. She felt like telling him to stuff them up his alb, but only for a fleeting second. Nobody ever spoke like that to a priest. Then he added her mother, asking when the babies' baptisms would be.

"I don't know, Father, she isn't up and about yet."

"Well, tell her not to leave it too late."

Did he know something she didn't? Had he a second sense about little Rebecca? Her mother did seem worried about her. He turned to speak to another parishioner and she and her grandfather carried on.

Several friends came over to speak to them, many of them recognising Gampy and asking him questions, but not smiling boy. After one more glance around to see if he could be lurking, she pulled her grandfather away.

He appeared to limp as they made their way home. "It's nothing," he replied when she remarked on it.

Should she worry about him as well as baby Rebecca? He was old, but she had heard of people living well into their seventies and there had even been one lady down the street who had been eighty-four when she had died, so he should have plenty of time left. It would be unbearable to lose another loved one. Gampy dying, she hated to admit, would be more devastating than her father's death. 'No, no, Papa, I didn't mean that,' she yelled inwardly. 'It just came into my head, without me knowing.' *Oh, 'eck, now I've done it.* One shouldn't speak ill of the dead. Or think ill.

Realising she had gone a long way ahead, she slowed down as she came to the park gates and waited for him. "Shall we sit in here for a while, Gampy, so you can rest?"

He nodded. Several people were out enjoying the Sunday sun but she spotted an empty bench and they sat down.

He rubbed his hands together. "Brr, it's cold."

Ignoring the chilblains on her fingers, she took his hands in hers and rubbed them. "I'd have thought your skin would be toughened by being at sea."

"My kith and kin may be, but my..." He hesitated as if thinking. "My soil and mud ain't as thick as it used to be."

"Your what?" She tried to work out what he had meant. "Ah, blood. Gampy, you've just made that up again."

He chuckled. "If you can't think of the proper rhyme, then devise your own, that's what I say."

"Did you use this peculiar language at sea?"

"No, no need for it there. We had our own particular way of speaking."

"Why do you feel the need for it now?"

He shrugged, giving her a smile.

Wrapping her scarf around her neck more tightly, she stood up. "Anyway, we'd better return home. Mama might need us. And I suppose I'd better see Missus Edwards from next door to check on little Tommy."

"I wonder where he came from," he replied as she helped him up. "Tell me again what the woman said."

She racked her brain. So much had happened since that fateful day, it had all become a blur.

"You said she asked if Bill were home."

"Yes. Who could she have meant?"

"She must have been deluded or demented."

"Well, she must have been insane to leave her baby like that. I've never had one, but I'm sure I wouldn't want to abandon it."

"She may not have wanted to. People do peculiar things when they're desperate."

They walked the remainder of the way home in silence, each lost in their own thoughts. Harriet could hear him puffing and panting. Maybe it had been too far for him, but she hadn't realised how infirm he had become. He'd had no problem going to The Princess the other night. But then, she hadn't gone with him, and maybe he had.

Settling him with a slice of bread and cheese and a cup of tea, after checking on her mother, who had fed the babies again, and sat reading a magazine, she told him she was going next door.

He lit up his pipe.

"That doesn't help with your breathing, Gampy. Maybe you should give it up," she admonished him.

The reply he gave, although she may have misheard him, was not what a lady should hear.

Missus Edwards from next door greeted her with tears in her eyes. "Harriet, I was about to come round."

"Is there something wrong with Tommy?"

"No, no, he's thriving, and I give him ordinary boiled milk, so I don't have to bother Missus Leekes."

He lay in the perambulator, gurgling and kicking his chubby legs. "He seems to have put on weight."

Missus Edwards covered him up and sniffed in Harriet's ear. "But I can't have him any longer," she surprised her by sobbing.

"Oh."

"It isn't that I don't want to, mind you. No, not at all."

Harriet swallowed. She'd been hoping the lady would keep him, especially with the arrival of the twins.

"It's my old man, you see. He says..." She blew her nose as tears poured down her face. "He says as how we can't afford him. He's lost his job, see, and, anyway, Mark don't like him, and says he never will." Sobbing once more, she covered her face with a grubby handkerchief from her apron pocket.

Harriet patted the neighbour's back, but she was inconsolable. "It's fine, Missus Edwards. I'll take him. Now Mama's home, we'll manage." That didn't help, though. "And I'll bring him round for you to cuddle whenever you want."

"No...that would...make it...worse," she muttered between sobs.

Heavy footsteps came down the stairs. Harriet had hoped to be away before Mister Edwards appeared, but he walked in, his braces hanging down, with only a grimy vest covering his upper half.

Harriet expected him to shout at his wife, but he put his arms around her. "Don't upset yourself so, Mary. You always knew it was a temporary arrangement."

"Yes," agreed Harriet. "I hadn't expected you to keep him forever." Maybe hoped. "Shall I take him now?"

Mister Edwards nodded.

With Missus Edwards's cries rending the still air, Harriet opened the front door and manoeuvred the perambulator outside. She pushed it up the ginnel between the houses and parked it outside the back door, making sure Tommy was fully covered, before going inside.

Her grandfather had fallen asleep in the armchair, so she crept upstairs. Her mother sat up when she opened the door. "Hello, dearie, is everything well? You look troubled."

"I'm fine, Mama, it's…" Should she tell her now or wait until later?

"Come on, out with it. I may be abed but I can still function as your mother."

"It's baby Tommy, Mama. We have to have him back." She told her what had happened.

"I thought I could hear someone crying. Ah, well, only one more mouth to feed."

"But, how will you manage when I'm at work?"

"Your grandfather will help."

"But…" She thought better of telling her of her concerns over him. "Are you sure?"

"Well, my dearie, worse things have happened at sea, so they say."

Harriet laughed. "I'll bet Gampy has said that a few times."

"We'll cope. Us Londoners always do. We're a hardy bunch. I'm sure someone, either Missus Bowe or Missus Leekes or someone will help."

"Missus Edwards from next door says he can take ordinary milk now. I'll check if we have enough to last 'til tomorrow. Would you like anything bringing up, 'cos I might go and see Lucy?"

"No, dearie, I'm fine, thank you. What have you done with baby Tommy?"

"He's outside in his perambulator. Do you think I should bring him in?"

Her mother took a look outside. "No, it seems pretty fair out there. As long as he's well wrapped up, the fresh air will do him good. Um…by the way," she pointed under the bed, "my po could do with emptying, if you wouldn't mind."

After emptying the chamber pot into the outside privy, and checking that baby Tommy wouldn't catch cold, she went to the Bowes' house.

"I'll bet Missus Edwards handed him back because she was scared she might murder him," declared Lucy when Harriet informed her of everything that had happened since the last time they had spoken.

"No, I don't believe that at all. She was heart-broken. Anyway, do you fancy going for a walk, to the park or somewhere?"

"But have you told your grandfather about baby Tommy being outside the back door. What if he wakes up and hears cries? Won't he be anxious?" Lucy asked as she put on her coat and scarf.

"Oh, yes. We'll tell him before we go, even if we have to wake him. Gampy, that is, not the baby."

Her grandfather still snored in the armchair, so they decided to take Tommy with them. "Hopefully, he'll sleep all the way, so he'll be no trouble," she assured Lucy.

"Well, if he starts crying, I'm off. I can't be doing with screaming infants," Lucy replied.

"You might have some of your own one day."

"I can hardly wait."

Harriet looked at her friend askance. "Don't you want children of your own?"

"Not really. I'm sure I'll manage without."

"But that's unnatural."

Lucy shrugged. "Maybe it is, but I can't help my feelings. Don't tell Mama, though. The one time I mentioned it to her, she hit the roof."

"I'm not surprised. But you seemed to be happy when I first brought Tommy to your house."

Lucy opened the park gates. "That was different. He isn't mine. I wonder if we'll meet any eligible bachelors today." She glanced down at the perambulator. "Probably not, with that monstrosity to put off possible suitors."

107

Harriet stopped. "Lucy, if you're so peeved at walking with me, I wonder you came at all."

"Take no notice of me. It's that time of the month. I always get crotchety when my fairies are present."

"Say, you can tell me, for my mother just made me more confused when she explained about babies. Tell me, do you know how they get into their mother's belly?"

Lucy's face turned bright red and she stopped, not lifting her head, whispering, "We can't speak about that here. Someone may hear us, and it's not the sort of thing young ladies talk about." She gasped, "Oo, Harriet, just look over there. It's that young man I told you about. The one I saw last time I came."

"Which one, the tall one with the top hat, or the other one with the red coat?"

"The red coat. Isn't he gorgeous? Don't let him see us staring. Look the other way."

Harriet pretended to tuck up the baby, whilst sneakily peeking under her eyebrows at the beau. "He's rather old, isn't he?"

"Maybe for you, but you forget, I'm nearly sixteen."

"But he would probably want babies. Would you tell him you don't?"

"Don't be ridiculous. Of course not. I should have to catch him first. Oo, my, stop! He's coming closer."

"Do you want me to walk away?"

Lucy grabbed her sleeve. "No, don't leave me on my own."

But she had just declared that having the perambulator would put young men off, so why did she insist on her staying?

The two men walked past without a glance in their direction or a break in their conversation.

"He looked at me, didn't he?" gushed Lucy, once they were out of earshot.

"Did he? I didn't notice."

"Well, you wouldn't. You're too young."

And too blind, evidently.

"Oo, he's dreamy. I wonder if they'll turn back." Lucy watched the men go out through the gates. "Ah, it doesn't seem like it. What rotten luck. But at least I've seen him. What do you think his name could be?"

Harriet laughed. "How would I know? What name would you like him to have?"

"Um, something like…" She pulled a face, the cogs in her brain clearly clicking round. "Arthur? Do you like that?"

"Not particularly. How about…Oliver, as in that book about the orphan boy?"

"Now you're being silly. Why would I want a suitor to have the same name as an orphan?"

"I just like the name. I might call my first baby Oliver."

"But what if it's a girl, eh? Then what would you call it?"

"Olivia?"

"I'm bored with this game. Oo, what a handsome pair of horses."

Harriet had seen the black horses pulling a fancy carriage, with a lady and a man, dressed in the height of fashion, inside. She gasped. Miss Little and her husband, or rather, Mister and Missus Lighten.

Should she acknowledge them or pretend not to have seen them? However, the decision was taken out of her hands when the carriage pulled to a halt a few yards away.

"Harriet, how good to see you taking the fresh air," called Miss Little. Her husband seemed eager to carry on, and he reached across her and instructed the driver to continue, but his wife continued, "Is that one of your baby brothers? Do let me see." She leaned over to take a look. Harriet thought she would fall out as the carriage picked up speed again. It passed by and she could hear her chuntering at her husband for not allowing her to see him.

"Who was that?" asked Lucy, watching them depart. "How do you know folk with carriages?"

"That, my dear friend, is my new employer, Miss Louisa Little."

As they continued their walk Lucy asked, "Ah, the haberdasher, but is she married to the gentleman?"

"Yes, but she had the shop before she was married and she prefers to keep her maiden name when associated with it. Apparently, it was his suggestion. He seems a bit of a tartar to me. He's much older than her. But you might like him. You seem to prefer older men."

"Tosh, not that old."

The baby opened his eyes. "He isn't going to cry, is he?" asked Lucy, peering inside the perambulator. "We'd better turn back if he is."

"Oh, dear, it looks like it. Dash it, I forgot to check if we had enough milk. What shall I do if we haven't? I can't buy any 'til tomorrow."

"We may have some spare, and if we haven't, you could go around the neighbours and ask for a cupful from each of them. That should be plenty." Lucy made pouring movements with her hands to demonstrate her meaning.

Harriet laughed. "Yes, I should think so."

"Or maybe your mama will have a little spare." She cupped her breast.

Embarrassed, Harriet nudged her arm away. "That's not very likely. She moans that she doesn't have enough. William Thomas likes a lot."

As they turned to go back Lucy remarked, "That's rather a mouthful, William Thomas, isn't it? Why don't you shorten it to Willy or something?"

"Papa doesn't...I mean, didn't, like us to shorten names, but I agree. Will would be better."

"Ah," Lucy glanced around at the people parading up and down, "there doesn't seem to be anybody left worth hanging about for."

Harriet pushed the perambulator faster when Tommy started to yell loudly. "Would you have stayed out on your own?"

"No, it would not be appropriate for a young lady to parade alone."

Harriet giggled. "I don't see any young ladies."

"You speak for yourself, but now you're a haberdashery assistant you can add yourself to that category."

They reached their street, and one or two curtains twitched as they ran by with the screaming infant.

"I may come round later," Harriet called as she ran up the passageway to the back door.

Her grandfather sat in the kitchen as she took in the baby. "My, my, what a noise. I suppose this is the foundling."

"Yes, Gampy." She spotted the milk jug and looked inside. "Please hold him a minute while I boil his milk." Without waiting for a reply, she thrust Tommy at him. "Do we have any more? This isn't enough." After pouring what was there into a saucepan, she put it on the range while she went into the pantry to find more. Fortunately, there was another bottle. How fortunate she had bought plenty.

"He has a good pair of lungs," remarked Gampy, trying to pacify him by jogging him up and down on his knee.

The milk heated, she then had to wait for it to cool. "It's coming, it's coming," she yelled, not that it stopped the wailing.

"Give him a biscuit," her grandfather told her. "That should shut him up."

"Is he allowed them?"

"I don't see why not. He's big enough, in my opinion."

Harriet took the lid off the biscuit barrel. One lonely scrap lay there, so she stuffed it in the baby's mouth. It shut him up until the milk cooled and she could make him porridge.

"What would I do without you, Gampy?" She put her arms around him and hugged him.

Her grandfather stretched. "I have my uses."

Chapter 16

When Harriet returned home from work she was surprised to see her mother downstairs. The smell of cooking took her into the kitchen and she lifted the lid off a pan of stew and sniffed the delicious aroma.

Her ma followed her and sat at the table. "Just what the doctor ordered. Not that we can afford one of them. I thought the midwife would have been back. She hasn't been since... Um...it was only yesterday, wasn't it? No, what day is it? Monday. I mean Saturday."

Harriet laughed at her confusion as Gampy dished out the meal.

In between mouthfuls she asked Harriet, "How was your day at work, dear?"

"Very good," replied Harriet. "I'll tell you about it when I've finished this delicious repast."

"Ooer, where did you learn to use such fine words?"

"It must be Miss Little's influence. She's very well-spoken."

They all looked up, surprised, when a knock came on the door. "Who the heck can that be?" grumbled Gampy.

Harriet opened the door. By the light of the flickering candles she made out a young woman, dressed in a shabby, dark-coloured dress, with rips in the lace, clinging onto a shawl wrapped around her head. She turned with big round eyes.

"Who is it, dearie?" called her mother. "Let them in out of the cold. What are you thinking, leaving visitors on the doorstep?"

Harriet stepped aside for the woman to enter. "You're the one who dumped the baby, aren't you?"

The woman nodded. "'Ow is 'e?"

"Well, young lady, you have a cheek to come waltzing in here like this," moaned Gampy, picking up his pipe. The shawl covering the woman's head dropped down. "Why, you're only a scrap of a girl," he exclaimed. "But I want to know why you left your child and ran off without an explanation."

With tears falling down her grimy cheeks, the girl looked inside the perambulator and stroked the baby's cheek. "It were either that or let 'im starve."

"But why leave him here?"

The girl went over to the mantelpiece and picked up a photo. "This is Billy, i'n't it?"

Harriet snatched it from her. "No. There isn't anybody in this house called Billy, so sling your hook, and take your snotty baby with you."

"Harriet!" cried her mother. "Don't be so rude."

"Well, she swans in here, dumps her brat on us and it isn't even the right house."

Gampy took the photo and showed it to the girl. "Which one are you calling Billy?"

She pointed to William Henry.

"Ah," he said. "Billy's short for William, of course. I'm known as Sailor Bill down the docks."

"But...?" began Harriet. "Are you saying you knew my brother?"

The girl looked surprised. "Brover?"

"Yes, William was my brother."

"Was? Why you saying was?"

"Are you telling me our William is the father of your baby?" demanded Gampy. "Is that what you mean?"

With a worried expression, she nodded.

"Well, my brother's dead, so you can take your brat..." Harriet stopped at her ma's intake of breath.

"Harriet, why are you being so horrible?"

"Because..." She slumped onto the sofa. "I don't know, I just..."

"Anyway, my dear," Gampy turned back to the girl, "what's your name?"

"Agnes."

"Well, Agnes, what were your intentions in coming here today?"

"I just wanted to see 'im." Tears fell down her cheeks as she stroked the baby's cheek again. "I miss 'im so much. 'E looks fatter."

"That's because we've fed him," sneered Harriet, still peeved.

"I 'ad no money."

"Let's get this straight," said Gampy as he replaced the photo. "You say my grandson is the father of your child? So why haven't you been in touch before? Why wait until now, now he's dead, to come forward?"

"I didn't know 'e were dead. I ain't seen 'im fer months."

"That's probably because he enlisted, and he's been living in Aldershot," chipped in Harriet.

"'E told me 'e wanted to be a soldier."

"How did you meet him?"

"'E used to come to my 'ouse. Him and my brover was pals."

"So you thought you'd found a nice rich boy, a meal ticket?" sneered Harriet. "But he wasn't rich, was he?"

"No, it weren't nothink like that. I...we..." The girl looked as if she were about to faint.

"Harriet, let the girl sit down," said her mother. "She doesn't appear to have had a decent meal in ages. Is there any of that stew left?"

"Mama!"

"Don't bovver wiv me, Missus," whispered Agnes, although she sat down.

Gampy went into the kitchen and came back with his plate. "Here, girl, I couldn't eat all mine. You have it."

The girl stared at it for a moment and then tucked in. The food only lasted a few seconds.

He went back for the remains of Harriet's food. "Do you want this, Harriet?"

She shook her head and the girl scoffed that as well.

"So where is your brother now? And your parents? You look as if you've been living on the streets," Gampy continued.

"My brover joined up. That must be what gave Billy the idea, but 'e stopped comin' round, and I only found out the other week where 'e lived. You see, me ma kicked me out when I 'ad the baby."

"Your own mother?"

Agnes nodded.

"So, where have you been living all this while, and didn't your father say anything?"

"Pa upped and left a year ago, wiv some floozie from down the street. I ain't seen 'im since."

"My goodness, and do you have other brothers and sisters?"

"Yep, I got three sisters and two other brovers and me ma's expecting again. She's probably 'ad the kid by nah."

"But I thought you said your father…?"

"She found herself another bloke. I were glad in a way when she threw me out, 'cos I 'ate him. 'E's vile. 'E used to beat me up."

"You poor girl." Gampy sat staring into the fire.

Harriet held her breath, fearful that they were going to ask the girl to stay. She was probably flea-ridden, her long, dank hair crawling with lice.

"We called your baby Tommy after my little boy who died last year," she heard her mother say, matter-of-factly. "What name did you gave him?"

"William, or Billy for short, after 'is pa ."

"My baby boy's called that. How confusing. Have you had him christened?"

"No, I never got round to it."

"That's fine, then, we can carry on calling him Tommy. If that's all right with you?"

Why is she talking as if there's a future with this girl? She can't be considering keeping the baby? thought Harriet, turning her back on Agnes.

"It don't matter to me." Agnes stood up. "Um... I..."

"Sit down, girl," said Gampy. "If what you say is true, and that baby is really the son of my grandson, then, he's staying here, and you with him."

Harriet couldn't bite her tongue any longer. "But, Gampy, where would she sleep?"

"She can have my bed. I'll sleep down here."

Wringing her tatty-gloved hands Agnes turned to stare at him. "No. I'll doss in a doorway. I'm used to doin' that."

Harriet shook her head as her mother added, "You're doing no such thing but, no offence, dearie, you'll have to take a bath. I'll fill the copper for hot water."

Gampy jumped up. "No, you won't."

"But, Pa, look at the state of her."

"I'll do it. You should be in bed, not lifting things."

With a shake of her head, Harriet turned up her nose. "I'm going to Lucy's." She grabbed her coat from the back of the door, and went out before she'd finished putting it on.

Chapter 17

Harriet sat in the Bowe's house, bemoaning her lot. "She's a trollop, only a little older than me, and there they are, welcoming her like the prodigal son."

Lucy patted her hand. "I suppose, if baby Tommy is really your brother's son, they feel obliged."

"Yes, but there's no need to have her in the house as well."

Missus Bowe looked up from her sewing. "I thought you Catholics preached good will to all men and that sort of thing. Your attitude isn't very christian."

The woman was right. She should feel compassion for the wretched girl.

"And it is nearly Christmas," added Lucy. She searched behind the sofa and brought out a half-knitted sock. "I'm making these for my pa."

Harriet remembered the card she had been making for her father. There wouldn't be any point finishing it. "I'm sure he'll love them," she said dejectedly.

"What…? Oh, I'm sorry, babbling on about my pa, when yours is…" Lucy shoved the knitting where she'd found it. "What about your ma, what are you making her?"

"I've just done a little tapestry. But I haven't made anything for the twins. They weren't due 'til after Christmas. Or Gampy. I didn't know he'd be home. What with everything that's happened, it all slipped my mind. What am I going to do?" She burst into tears.

Lucy put her arm around her. "I'll help you. What sort of thing would you like to make?"

"You know I'm useless at knitting, so I can't make them even a pair of bootees," she wailed.

"Don't fret yourself, girlie," replied Missus Bowe, her needles seeming to fly. "I'll help you. It won't take two minutes to run up a pair each. But your grandfather, now he's a different matter."

"I should be paid on Friday so I can buy him some tobacco or maybe, a new pipe, if I've earned enough. But I promised to give him all my wages for the household bills."

"Ask him if you could keep some to buy presents," suggested Lucy. "Don't say who for."

Harriet wiped her eyes on her sleeve. "Yes. Thank you. I'm glad I came."

"Shall we play a game?"

"But don't you want to finish your pa's sock while he's not here?"

Lucy glanced across at her mother who replied, "Don't ask me to do it. I've just taken on more work." As Harriet began to protest, she continued, "More knitting. I don't mean work. It's a pleasure to help you, my dear, and I'll really enjoy the task. It's a long time since I made baby clothes and could be a while until Lucy here has one, if ever."

Harriet remembered their conversation the previous day. "She'll probably change her mind when she's older, but surely your other children have babies?"

"Not any more. They're all toddlers or older."

She recalled children playing outside the house a few days before. "Are they all coming at Christmas?"

"Not all, I hope," laughed Missus Bowe. "We'd be a touch overcrowded with all nineteen of them." She stretched and yawned. "I'm off to my bed. Don't make too much noise playing your games."

"We won't, Mama," chimed Lucy, dealing out the cards.

"We'd better not play Snap, or even Happy Families, for that can be rowdy," added Harriet.

Lucy picked up her hand. "It does when my nieces and nephews play."

"What are we playing?" whispered Harriet as Missus Bowe climbed the stairs, her arthritic hip making it difficult.

119

Lucy laughed. "Didn't I say? Old Maid."

"That's a good start. I have her already."

"I'd better be careful which one I choose then." Lucy didn't pick that card and Harriet ended up losing. "Shall we play cribbage now?" She could see her friend yawning, and knew she should be going home, but that girl, that Agnes, might still be there.

"I'm really sorry, Hattie," said her friend, yawning once more, and reminding Harriet of the diminutive name she used to be called when she was little. "But I'm so tired I could fall asleep in my chair."

"I'm being selfish." Harriet stood up. "Of course. It's just that..."

"If she is still there," her friend must have read her mind, "you'll have to grin and bear it. She may be a very nice girl. If she were in love with your brother she must have some redeeming qualities." Lucy helped her into her coat.

"She never said they were in love."

"Well, if she's had his baby, they must have been, unless your brother was the most dissolute rake imaginable, and neither of us thinks that." Lucy opened the door and practically shoved Harriet through it. "Good night. I'll wait with bated breath to hear what happens. Come round after dinner tomorrow."

Harriet had nothing for it but to return home. With sluggish gait, she entered the house.

A pretty young girl with blue eyes, fair hair and perfect skin—not like her, with the birthmark on her right cheek and her roman nose—sat on the sofa, dressed in one of her mother's old frocks, feeding baby Tommy a bottle. Could it be the same girl? Taken aback, she stood holding the door open.

"Put the wood in the hole," called her grandfather from inside the kitchen. "You're letting out all the irish peat."

He must be in a good mood, to be using his rhyming words again, she thought. "I'm sorry, Gampy," she replied, still staring at the girl. Was it Agnes? It had to be. They wouldn't have invited another girl in, but where had all the grime and dirt gone? "I'm going to bed."

"You can have your bedroom back now."

Harriet looked hopefully at Agnes. "But…"

"She can share with you. The bed's big enough."

"Um, no thanks. Mama still needs me to keep her company."

"Well, don't disturb your mother then." He smiled at Agnes. "When he's finished, put him in his pram. He can sleep down here with me."

"Goodnight, Gampy." She wasn't going to acknowledge the girl.

"Goodnight." He didn't even look at her as she went up the stairs. So much for being his favourite person in the whole world. It appeared she had been usurped, or whatever the word was. Hopefully, once the girl had fed Tommy, she'd go. Where to, she didn't care, as long as it was far away.

However, when she went downstairs the following morning, ready for work, she heard movements in the kitchen. It couldn't be her mother, for she had left her asleep, and her grandfather lay snoring on the sofa. She tiptoed through, thinking she might catch the girl doing something wrong. What that might be, she didn't know, but it would give her an excuse to be rid of her.

Lifting the teapot, Agnes asked, "Cuppa?" in such a quiet voice she could barely hear her.

She nodded. What else could she do? She sat at the table, fastening her boots.

"I were going to make porridge," added Agnes. "Would you like some?"

121

"I don't have time." A plate of porridge would have been welcome, but she wasn't about to pander to the girl. She'd rather starve.

"Your ma and grandpa said I can stay for a while. Yer don't mind, do yer?"

Mind? She was furious. But at least she'd be at work all day, earning money to pay for her keep. What did this girl contribute to the household, but her illegitimate brat? Although it wasn't the baby's fault. He was rather cute. "Are you going to find a job, then?"

"Um, yes, of course."

"I found my own job. I went out and found it, myself. I didn't wait for it to come to me." For some unknown reason, Harriet found herself speaking precisely and slowly as if to a child.

Her grandfather came through, his nightcap skew-whiff. "Good day, ladies. I hope you're becoming acquainted." He looked pointedly at Harriet, as if he'd heard what she'd been saying.

She merely replied, "I'm off to work," and tipped up her cup to finish the tea. It was much too strong for her liking, and she pulled a face.

"Have you had breakfast? You shouldn't go out in this cold weather without something hot inside you."

"This strong tea will do, Gampy. That's hot." She kissed his cheek and went out the back door, so as not to wake Tommy.

Her stomach making all sorts of peculiar noises as she walked the mile to work, she regretted her decision. If Miss Little didn't offered to take her out for lunch, like on the previous day, she'd go hungry for the whole day. Sighing, she regretted the stubborn side to her nature. Her papa had always said it would land her in difficulties one day.

Arriving at the shop much too early, she trudged up and down the street, comparing other shop windows to theirs, and deciding they weren't nearly as delightful. She had forgotten her shawl, had just pulled on her coat, in her hurry to leave. Her bonnet didn't keep out the wind that blew from the top of the street, seeming to come to a climax right outside the shop.

Clapping her hands did not help, nor stamping her feet, so by the time Miss Little hurried towards her, apologising for keeping her waiting, she knew what an icicle must feel like. Cold and shivery, she could barely move. Miss Little lit the fire and put the kettle on to boil while she watched, fearful she'd die of a chill.

"Come over here, child. Tell me why you're so cold." Miss Little rubbed her hands between hers.

It all seemed petty in the light of day. What would her papa have said about her outrageous behaviour?

She explained what had happened.

Miss Little listened with interest while she poured out the tea. "But, surely that's a good thing, that the little boy has been reunited with his mother? You don't seem pleased."

"I'm being silly. I should welcome her with open arms, but… Gampy seems to like her more than me."

"Ah, the green-eyed monster." She turned the CLOSED sign to OPEN and peeped outside. No customers were waiting; she went back to Harriet. "You've been the apple of your grandfather's eye all your life, and you think this Agnes will usurp you in his affections?"

She had used the right word earlier. That pleased her. "Something like that."

"Well, she won't, I assure you. He is being protective. If she has been living rough, she must be in dire straits. You should be happy to have such a thoughtful and lovely grandfather."

"I am. As I said, I'm a silly goose. Ignore me." Harriet went through to the shop and picked up a pair of scissors that had been left out the previous night. They fell out of her hands as if she'd been burnt. Visions of sticking them into Agnes's chest had flitted through her mind. How depraved had she come! *Papa, please save me or I'll end up in Hell.*

"How is the storeroom coming along?" asked Miss Little, after Harriet had changed her dress.

"It's almost finished. You'll see a difference by the end of today," she replied in a monotone.

"Cheer up, my dear. Think of all those people who have no grandfather to love them; how deprived they must be."

"I know, I know. Do you have one?" she called as an afterthought.

"Yes, my father's father. He lives up in the wilds of Derbyshire, and I rarely see him. Count your blessings that yours is there everyday for you." Miss Little lined up the rolls of silk. "We must make sure all your hard work has not come to naught, and maintain the level of tidiness in the shop, as well as the back room. I can't believe how neat it looks since you had a go at it. Thank you."

Puffing out her chest, Harriet went into the back in a much lighter mood than when she had arrived.

Dust from layers of materials and boxes of ribbons that had not been touched, seemingly for years, made her sneeze, not just once, but so many times Miss Little ran in.

"Dear me, I hope you're not coming down with something."

"No, its…" sneeze, "just the…" sneeze, "dust."

She thought she'd had a handkerchief in her apron pocket, but grubbling about, she couldn't find it. Miss Little handed her one from her own pocket. Even after blowing her nose they wouldn't stop and, when the door bell tinkled, indicating a customer, Miss Little had to go through to the shop. Several sneezes later, weak at the knees, Harriet sat on a box, her head aching, and remembering what she had thought earlier about dying from a chill. She pulled the collar of her dress up over her throat, finding no other way to keep out the cold. Eventually they stopped and she relaxed.

A hot drink would help. As she poured tealeaves into the pot, she tried to make sense of her erratic behaviour. Why did she resent the girl so much? Could it be something to do with her brother not telling her? They used to be that close they didn't have secrets from each other. But she'd had no inkling about his involvement with Agnes, none at all.

"I hear they've stopped," Miss Louisa remarked on entering.

"Thank goodness. I've never sneezed so much in my life."

"Hopefully it's only the dust."

"Please God. I don't want anything more serious, not when I've only just started here. One of my neighbours died from diphtheria not long ago. You don't think it could be that, do you?"

"No, no, child. My mother, God rest her soul, died from the disease, and I don't recall her having the sneezes, just a fever and a very sore throat."

"I'm sorry. I didn't know that." Harriet swallowed a few times to make sure her throat didn't hurt.

"That reminds me, she had the same name as you. I wonder if we are related."

"I doubt it, ma'am. How could my poor family be related to yours?"

"Didn't you tell me they were not always so poor?"

"Yes, but…"

"I feel such an affinity to you, dear Harriet, that it would not be beyond the realms of possibility." As she went to serve another customer she added, "Ask your grandfather for the details of his parents and grandparents."

She's serious, though Harriet. *Wouldn't it be wonderful if we found we were cousins of some sort?* On that thought, she continued her work with renewed energy.

Determined to find out, she hurried home, skirting around the street vendors, even though some of their wares smelled delicious.

Forcing a smile to her lips, she went through the front door, to be greeted by her mother. "Come and warm yourself, my dearie."

Pleasantly surprised to see nobody else there, she thought better of asking if the girl had gone, and decided to enjoy the moment of peace. "Should you be out of bed, Mama?" She hugged her.

"I can't stay up there all day long. I'd go mental. As long as I don't do too much, I'll be fine."

"Is baby...? Did we decide on Rebecca in the end?" Guilt coursed through Harriet as she realised she hadn't seen much of the twins since the day they were born, apart from peering at them in their drawers when she went to bed or before work.

"Yes, although I'd prefer them both to have names that start with the same letter, and as we've agreed on William Thomas for the boy, can you think of a girl's name beginning with W?"

"Wilemena?" suggested Harriet as she took off her coat and hung it on the back of the door.

Her mother shook her head. "No, it's too much like William. Your grandfather thought of Wendy."

"I haven't heard of that. Where is he, by the way?" Should she ask about the other person?

"He went for a walk..." Her mother hesitated. "He went for a walk with Agnes and Tommy."

Of course, the perambulator had gone. *Probably to make sure she was out of the way when I arrived,* she thought.

Her mother put a pan on the range. "They should be back shortly."

Harriet took out four knives and forks to lay the table. "Anyway, how about Winifred? We could call her Winnie, for short; or Watson, we could call her Watty; or Wilson, we could...."

"Now you're being silly. Watson and Wilson are boys' names. It'll have to be Winifred. Would you like her to have a second name like yours, Loxley?"

"Loxley, after your mother, yes, that'd be wonderful." As long as it wasn't Agnes. "By the way, Miss Louisa has asked me to find out what Gampy's parents names were." She went on explain what her employer had suggested.

"But Gampy's name's Bond. It'd be your father's father whose name we'd need and, as your father was a foundling, we don't know if Harding was his real name."

"Oh, yes. Did I tell you her husband's name?" At her mother's shake of the head, she continued with a giggle, "Lancelot."

"Like in those stories about King Arthur?"

"Yes, but I wouldn't call him a knight. He seems... How can I put it? Well, not very agreeable."

"Miss Little must love him," replied her mother, sitting down and resting her arms on the table.

Harriet tried to pull her up. "Mama, why don't you go back to bed?"

"I'm fed up with my bed, that's why. I'll be fine." She leant her head on her arms.

"I'll finish dinner. You sit on the sofa." She tried once more, but her mother wouldn't budge.

A squall of wind blew in from the front door as her grandfather and his new friend entered, dragging the baby carriage behind them. They were giggling. Her Gampy rarely giggled. How unfair!

"Ah, Hattie," he grinned at her. How odd! Lucy had called her that the previous evening. "We were..."

She didn't want to know what they'd been doing, and interrupted him with, "Dinners almost ready, Gampy," muttering under her breath, "Good day to you, too."

At the judgemental set of his face, she turned back to the kitchen.

Her mother looked up. "Is that your grandfather?"

"Yes, Mama. Shall I dish out the dinner?"

"Yes, please, if you would. I'd help, but…"

"No, no, Mama, you sit there. I can manage."

How should she divide out the food? Her mother should have the biggest portion, because she needed the energy to feed two babies; her grandfather the next biggest, because he was a man; she herself the next; that left a small spoonful of scrapings for the newcomer.

They sat down and Gampy said grace. He noticed the difference in portions and, giving Harriet a long glare from under his bushy eyebrows, said, "Is that all there is? Couldn't you find a little more for our guest?"

Her fork halfway to her mouth, she replied, "She's welcome to scrape out the pan. It's over there." She put the potato into her mouth and chewed with exaggerated motions.

Agnes shook her head. "This is loads. Don't bovver 'bout me."

"You need to build up your strength, Agnes." He fetched the saucepan. "Um, there doesn't seem to be any left." Spooning some off his own plate, he added, "Here, I have too much, take some of mine."

Her mother copied him. "Me, too. I shall never eat all this."

Head down, so she couldn't tell if her grandfather was scowling at her, Harriet continued eating. She didn't have an excessive portion, and would easily finish it. Anyway, the girl had more than her by that point.

They finished the meal in silence and Agnes jumped up to clear the plates. Harriet allowed her to do it. Since she had become the breadwinner, she shouldn't have to wash them.

Her mother pushed herself away from the table. "If you don't mind, my dearies, I shall leave you to it."

She could hardly walk, so Harriet took her arm. "Let me help you, Mama. I knew you should have gone back to bed earlier."

Her grandfather took her other arm, muttering, "Stubborn as a mule, the whole family."

Once she had made sure her mother was tucked up in bed, she padded over to her newest brother and sister, sleeping contentedly. So enfolded in their swaddling clothes, she could only see their little faces, and she still couldn't tell William from Winifred, or Winnie, as she had decided to call her. She stroked the cheek of the one she thought must be the girl, disturbing her. She jumped back, whispering, "No, please don't wake up. Mama's only just gone to sleep, and I can't feed you." Luckily, she settled down again and, with a sigh of relief, Harriet went downstairs.

The kitchen neat and tidy, she sat next to their visitor, keeping a distance between them. Her grandfather watched them from beneath his bushy eyebrows, smoking his pipe, reminding her that she needed to ask him something. "Gampy?"

"Yes, child?"

"You know when I'm paid my *wages* on Friday for *working*?" She emphasised the important words, so the girl beside her knew her place.

He nodded, taking another puff.

"Well, would I be able to keep a few pennies to buy presents?"

"Of course, child. We hadn't come to any arrangement."

That had been easier than she'd anticipated. "Thank you, thank you."

Agnes sat beside her, picking at the skin on the side of her still-grimy fingernails. Against her better judgement,

Harriet couldn't prevent a little sympathy for the girl. How would she give presents, with no money or means of making them? If Gampy and Mama looked after Tommy, she could find herself a job. There were plenty out there, if she looked hard enough.

She must have read her mind for she mumbled, "Tomorrow I'll look for work. I don't want to be no burden."

"How long are you staying?" asked Harriet.

Agnes glanced across at Gampy and then back to her hands.

Her grandfather cut in. "She's staying as long as she wants."

The back door opened and Missus Edwards from next door came in. "I hope I'm not putting you out, but I just wanted…Tommy, is he…?" She stopped on seeing Agnes. "I'm sorry I didn't realise you had a visitor."

Of course, the woman didn't know she'd turned up. "This is Tommy's mother," Harriet blurted out. "She arrived yesterday."

The woman's eyes seemed to grow larger and larger and her one tooth more obvious. "Oh, oh, I see."

Harriet turned to Agnes. "You nearly lost your baby to Missus Edwards here. She wanted to keep him. She was minding him for me, while Mama…" Why was she explaining things? The girl had abandoned Tommy. What right did she have to know?

"So?" began Missus Edwards "Are you taking him?"

Agnes, in her usual quiet voice, shrugged and mumbled, "I don't know what's 'appnin' yet."

Gampy sat back in his chair. "The girl is staying as long as she wants, as I keep saying. She is the mother of my great grandson."

The neighbour could not have appeared more surprised, "Your great grandson, but I don't understand."

"Missus Edwards," he replied, "Tommy is apparently the son of my grandson, William, and is as welcome to remain here as any of my family."

The lady peeped into the perambulator where Tommy lay kicking. "That's a happy ending, then. I don't suppose I could give him a cuddle, could I? I've missed him so much."

Agnes stood up. "'course, Missus." She put him in her arms. The look of ecstasy on the lady's face as she cuddled him melted Harriet's heart. How could one woman have that much love to give, and be damned? It didn't seem fair, and how could those gossip-mongers think she murdered her own son, when she reacted to Tommy in such a way?

The lady handed him back and, with tears in her eyes, went out, saying, "Please give my regards to your mother. I hope she's well."

"She is, thank you," replied Harriet. "Good day." The woman's sobs could be heard even after she had closed the door behind her. "Isn't it sad she can't have more children? She obviously loves them. It doesn't seem right that people who don't or shouldn't have them, do, and others who long so desperately for them don't." Not wanting to cause another argument, she daren't look at the girl beside her.

"That's the way of life, my girl," answered her grandfather. "You'll find that as you grow older. Life isn't fair for most people. It's a drudge, but we have to accept it and make the most of it."

"Aren't you going to make up one of your rhymes, Gampy?"

He smiled, for the first time that evening. Had it been her fault the atmosphere in the house had been dismal? Maybe she should try to accept the situation with more grace. It looked as if Agnes would be staying for the foreseeable future.

Chapter 18

Satisfied with her week's work, and hoping Miss Louisa would be, Harriet looked around the storeroom. The boxes were neatly stacked and labelled, some full of items for the sale they would have after Christmas, others with excess stock Miss Louisa had not realised she had. The drawers had been emptied and refilled tidily. Her employer had looked in occasionally, and remarked on how neat the shelves were, and how she could find at a glance whatever she had come in for.

Wiping dust from her hands, Harriet took a deep breath. She'd never imagined how rewarding a task could be. Never again would she allow it to drop to its cluttered standard.

"All finished," she declared, as she entered the shop.

Miss Louisa smiled. The customer whom she was serving looked familiar. But who would Harriet know that would come that far to buy ribbons? Then it dawned on her. The mother of the boy she fancied at church. Would the lady recognise her? Probably not, for she'd never spoken to her.

Adjusting her dress to look favourable, she advanced. She couldn't ask about him, for she didn't know his name. It would sound silly saying, "Good day, ma'am, how may I help you, and by the way, how is your son…um…thingamajig?"

The lady glanced at her and, for a second, seemed to recognise her but left without speaking.

"Harriet, what a wonder you are," declared Miss Louisa. "You have transformed my emporium into a place of beauty. That lady was only saying a moment ago what a delightful shop it is."

"Do you know her, Miss Louisa?"

"Why, no, it's her first visit. Your beautiful window display drew her in. She's coming back tomorrow when she has more money. Why? Do you know her?"

"Not really. She attends my church, and I sort of know her son."

"Only sort of?"

Harriet blushed, and opened a drawer as if to take something out. "Yes, I've never spoken to him. I just like him. He smiles at me sometimes."

"Ah, one of those long-distance attractions. I used to have those at your age."

Harriet tried to gauge her employer's age. She must have been staring, for Miss Louisa grinned. "I'm not that old I don't remember what it's like to think myself in love with a boy I don't know. How old do you think I am?"

Scared to offend, she bit the inside of her cheek. If she said she thought she was thirty, and it turned out that her assumptions were vastly inaccurate, the lady might sack her. "Twenty-five?" she offered.

"Ha, ha, well said, but I regret to say I left that age behind ten years or so ago."

"My mama turns forty next year. She says—or used to say before my pa died—that she'll be old and decrepit then. She probably feels so already."

"Don't say that. You'll make me feel old and decrepit."

"Miss Louisa, I didn't mean that. You have several years to go before…" Why didn't she keep her big mouth shut?

Miss Louisa patted her arm. "Don't worry about it."

"But you haven't had any babies yet."

Her employer gave her a peculiar look, but changed the subject. Was she upset that she might not have any? Or could it be something completely the opposite? Might she be expecting already? It would be imprudent to ask and she didn't want to put her foot in her mouth each time she opened it. Grinning at the thought of trying to work with her foot in her mouth, she felt her boot give, and looked

133

down to see a black-stockinged big toe poking through a hole.

Horrified, she pulled down her dress to hide it. The day before, she'd thought the leather was thin, but not that it would be delicate enough to break.

Maybe her mama had a pair of shoes hidden in the bottom of her wardrobe. Actually, since her mother would be confined for a few more weeks she could borrow hers. Their feet were about the same size, and it wouldn't be the first time they'd shared. Then again, she would be paid on the morrow. But she needed her first week's wage to buy her grandfather's Christmas present.

"Miss Louisa..." she began when the shop had once more emptied.

Her employer wiped her hand across her face. "I can't believe how busy we have been. Everyone says how the lovely window display enticed them to come inside. You're such an artistic girl, and that big silvery star hanging in the middle catches the light, and looks magic."

"Yet my mama tells me I'm a nincompoop because I can't knit."

"We can't all be good at everything, my dear. I can knit, and spend many an hour doing so, but would not know where to start designing such an exhibition."

"Yes, she does admit I can do other things. Anyway, would you happen to know how much clay pipes cost?"

Miss Louisa grinned. "Why? Are you thinking of taking up the habit?"

"No." With a bid to stop grinning again, she cast aside the image of herself smoking a pipe and blowing out the smoke. "I want to buy my grandfather a new one for Christmas and don't know if I'd have enough money. His old one looks like a sailor's head, because he's a sailor."

"Later on, take a gander in the pipe shop up the street. Not now, though, because I can see three ladies admiring your window and they might come in. Yes, yes," the door opened, "they are." She stood up straight and greeted the customers. "Good day, ladies, and what a fine day it is, too."

Harriet stepped back and tried to hide her foot, but soon forgot about it when more customers came in, and she became engaged in measuring ribbons and finding lace and hooks and eyes.

At closing time, they stood, hands on hips, flexing their backs, twisting to ease their aching necks.

"Well, my girl, you have done us proud, today." Miss Louisa opened the till and took out a wad of money. "I have never taken so much money in one day since I opened my little establishment." She reached into the drawer, took out a coin and wrapped Harriet's hand around it. "Here, take this as a thank you."

Thrilled, at first, Harriet expected to see a farthing, or maybe a halfpenny at the most, but when she opened her hand she gasped. "Um…Miss Louisa, is this my pay? I thought I wasn't having it 'til tomorrow and I…I hoped I'd have more than this." They hadn't actually discussed how much she would earn, but she knew pipes cost more than a shilling.

"No, silly, this isn't your wages. This is a bonus, something extra for being such a good and helpful assistant."

"I've never owned a whole shilling before. Is it all for me? Won't your husband think I've stolen it?"

"What has he to do with it? He need never know. And, anyway, he leaves the shop to me, as I've said before."

Harriet lifted up her skirt to show her big toe. "It'll go towards a new pair of boots."

"My child, you cannot walk around like that." Miss Louisa closed the door. "Come upstairs and we'll see if any of my old ones fit. You will not be offended if I offer them to you, would you?"

"Offended, ma'am? Not in the least, but your feet look much smaller than mine." Harriet tried to gauge the size as she followed her up the stairs. Did her foot fit on the stair fully, or did it overlap like hers? Miss Louisa took such delicate little steps she couldn't work it out.

"While we're at it, we'll see if there's another dress, so you don't have to wear the same one every day."

Full of glee and excitement, even with a big toe sticking out, she went up to the room they had visited before. Could it be only a few days ago? It seemed as if she'd been working there forever. Her grandfather often told her time passed more quickly the older one became, and it appeared to be so, even a week later. How grateful she was, not to be reciting the county towns and rivers of England and the capital cities of Europe and their rivers, every morning at school assembly. Some days they would learn how to form pot hooks and hangers to practise calligraphy on slates, using squeaky slate pencils or write the names of the kings and queens of England in their copybooks. Woe betide anyone who splodged ink on their work. The boys would be whacked by the cane on the back of the hand, while the girls received lines as punishment. One of her friends, who misbehaved all the time, had tied three pencils together, to finish them quicker.

Miss Louisa opened a drawer to reveal dainty shoes, some satin. "These are not appropriate, even if they fit you. They were my dancing shoes."

"You used to dance?" Harriet took out a soft, pink slipper.

"Yes, and sing. I had a vibrant mezzo-soprano voice in my youth," continued her employer, putting back the slipper and closing the drawer. "I performed at many a soirée."

Harriet marvelled at the many facets of Miss Louisa's life that she divulged each time they spoke intimately.

"Yes, my cousin, Jessie, used to accompany me on the pianoforte. She sang soprano, and could reach high notes with such a pure, clear voice. I wonder what happened to her. Her father and mine fell out and we haven't seen each other for..." Miss Louisa pulled at her lip, her brow furrowed in deliberation, "it must be nigh on ten years."

"I used to have an Auntie Jessie," said Harriet. "I suppose I still have, although I haven't seen her, either, since I was little. She married and moved to Yorkshire, or somewhere foreign."

Miss Louisa laughed. "Yorkshire isn't foreign. It's still in England."

"By the way, I meant to tell you, Mama says we can't be related as Papa was a foundling, and she doesn't know if his real name was Harding. It might have been the name of the family who took him in."

"Ah, that's a pity." She opened another drawer, containing sensible boots.

"Have you ever been to Yorkshire?" asked Harriet as she tried on one.

"No, I've never been out of London. How does that fit?"

She pulled a face. Much as she willed her foot to fit inside the brown leather boot, even with the laces loosened, it wouldn't. "Maybe the other one," she suggested.

"There's no point having one that fits and one that does not," smiled Miss Louisa as she handed her a different one. "What about this?"

Joy of joys, her foot slid in easily. The other pair would have suited her better, for they had softer leather, but not as practical. She would still have preferred them, but if she couldn't push her foot inside them, what would be the point? Should she suggest taking them to see if they suited her mother, in case her feet were slightly smaller? Would that be too bold? She decided not to push her luck. Maybe once her mother was up and about.

Miss Louisa opened the wardrobe to reveal the rack of dresses once more, and took out a light grey one. "This was my favourite." She held it against her and twirled around the tiny space. "I felt grand and beautiful when I wore this."

"But, Miss Louisa, you always look grand and beautiful," objected Harriet as she tried the other boot, "whatever you wear."

"Thank you, my child, for your kind words. I don't always feel so, especially since I... Anyway..." She replaced the frock and took out a burgundy one. "Would this be dark enough? I don't have another black one."

Harriet examined the dress, almost identical in style to the one she was wearing, with its high neck and full sleeves. "What do you think? Is it dark enough?"

"Well, I wouldn't wear it to church, but none of the customers know you are in mourning, so it would be all right to wear it here."

Would her papa and William mind if she didn't observe mourning? She stroked the soft material, longing to say she'd take it. To own two dresses would be beyond her wildest dreams, but to have one she couldn't wear would be torture. She handed it back. "May I ask Mama and Gampy first? Is that...?

"Yes, of course, my dear," replied Miss Louisa as she hung it up. "Don't worry about it. I'm sorry I didn't have the forethought to enjoy darker colours when I was gadding about in my earlier life."

Harriet stopped. Was she implying she was unthankful? "Miss Louisa, I am truly grateful, but... Should I take it to show them?"

"No, no, it will be an inconvenience. I didn't mean that as it sounded. Take no notice of me. How are the boots?"

"Wonderful, just wonderful. Thank you very much."

Skipping home, dangling the old holey boots in her hands, she felt like singing, and wondered what sort of voice she had, a soprano or whatever it was Miss Louisa's cousin had. How coincidental that her boss should have a cousin with the same name as her own aunty.

As she turned the corner of Hare Street she saw Isobel at her door. "What are you doing out here in the cold?" she asked the child.

"Waiting for my ma. She says she won't be long."

"Are you going somewhere nice?"

"Don't know. When can I come to your house again?"

"I'm not sure; what with all the babies and Gampy, it's a bit crowded."

Missus Leekes came out and closed the door behind her, moaning, "You can't trust a man for anything. All I want him to do is keep his ear out for John crying, and he says he will, but next minute he's snoring his head off in the armchair. But I ain't got time to change the baby. The shop'll be closed and I don't have enough in for dinner."

"We could lend you something," suggested Harriet. "I'm sure we'll have whatever you need."

"No, no, lass, thank you, anyway. You have enough mouths to cater for. If we hurry, Missus Green should still be open." She took Isobel's hand and scurried off, leaving Harriet wishing she had offered to look after Isobel for her so she could run quicker.

Old Mother Peele appeared behind her, making her jump. "You'll need your winter warmers on, girl. It's going to snow tomorrow, maybe even sooner, probably tonight," she warned before pulling her shawl over her head and dashing across the road between two horsemen. Everyone seemed to be in a hurry. Even the horses riding past appeared to clip-clop faster than usual.

Certain her unwelcome visitor would still be plonked on the sofa, draining their meagre resources, Harriet felt reluctant to return home. But, facing the inevitable, she trudged along as the old sage's words came true earlier than she had expected, and the first flakes of snow fell.

Be positive, she told herself as she opened the door. *Don't start an argument. Try to find good points in the situation.* Pinning a smile onto her lips, she breezed inside. "Aren't I a lucky girl?" She pointed her toe forward, to show off her new boots to whomever might be interested, but her grandfather was the only occupant of the room.

"Why, they're blood and sand, lass," he replied, peering at the proffered foot. "Where on earth did you buy them, and what with?"

Trying to balance on one foot, she glanced around. The perambulator still stood there in the corner, with baby Tommy gurgling, but no mother. Had she given up and left? "I didn't buy them, Gampy, and they are rather grand, aren't they?" Her balance deserting her, she put her foot down. "No, Miss Louisa gave them to me. Where's *she*?"

"Who? Miss Louisa? Surely you've only just left her?"

"No." She pointed to the sofa. "*Her.*"

"You mean my great-grandson's mother?"

So much for her earlier intention of positivity and good will. After taking off her coat, she decided to change the subject. "It's starting to snow, just like Old Mother Peele told me it would."

"I could have told you that, lass. You don't need to be going to that old paper bag for your weather forecasts."

"Paper bag? Ah, you mean wag?"

"Well, actually I didn't, I meant hag, but never mind. Going back to our previous conversation, *Agnes...*" he put extra inference on the name "has gone to the factory to find a dib and dob. She left hours ago, so I assume she found one."

"Or maybe she's done a runner." But no, that wouldn't make sense. She had fallen on her feet, landing on their doorstep, so she wouldn't want to leave any time soon.

"Why do you dislike her so much, girlie? It isn't at all like you."

She went to the kitchen to check on the dinner. "I don't know, Gampy. I just can't... Shall I take Mama a cup of tea? She must be awake for I can hear the floorboards creaking under her nursing chair."

His sigh could be heard behind her. "Yes, that'd be good. I'll have one as well."

The faint cry of a baby filtered down the stairs. "I bet that's William Thomas," she laughed. "He's a greedy little beggar, isn't he?"

Her grandfather did not reply straightaway but, looking into her eyes, he put his hand on her arm and said, "It's probably little Winnie. She's very poorly."

"What sort of poorly? Not poorly as in about-to-die poorly?"

His head wobbled, as if he couldn't decide whether to shake it or nod.

"I'd better go up. Is there anything I can do?" Without waiting for a reply, she ran up the stairs two at a time and pushed her mother's door open.

"Gampy just told me about Winnie. She isn't going to die, is she?"

Her mother looked up from the baby in her arms. "I'm praying she'll pull through, but she's so small, and has never fed well."

Harriet knelt beside her and stroked the baby's tiny hand. After a moment, it clenched around her finger. "Look, Mama, she's gripping me, so she must be all right."

"Let's pray it will be so."

They prayed for a few minutes until Gampy came in with a tray of tea. "How is she?" he asked as he set it down on the side table.

"About the same. She's stopped crying since Harriet came," her mother replied, smiling at her.

"May I hold her?" she asked. Her mother placed the baby in her arms. She sat on the bed, cuddling her and whispering in her ear, then looked up at the corner and

141

silently begged her father to ask God to make her better. Winnie fell asleep, and for a heart-stopping moment she thought she had joined him, but saw her little chest moving rhythmically under the layers of swaddling blankets.

Had it been her bad thoughts about Agnes that had caused the baby to be ill? Guilt washed over her as she cried, "I'm sorry, little one. If this is my fault, I shall never forgive myself."

Her cup in mid air her mother exclaimed, "How on earth can it be your fault, dearie? What makes you think that?"

Hiding her face in the baby's soft body, she squealed, "Because I've been so horrid to Agnes."

"But how can that make this little one ill?"

"I don't know, but she is and..." She looked up at the corner again, imagining her father to be frowning down on her. "It must be punishment." Tears poured down her cheeks at the result of her awful behaviour.

Her grandfather put his arm around her shoulder. "There's no way you should blame yourself, my little cockalorum. If I took the blame for every misdeed I'd performed, I...well, the whole universe would be dead by now."

"Oh, Gampy, you couldn't be that bad." She managed to smile though her tears.

The covers moved and her mother stood up and arched her back. "None of us is perfect, my darling, except for these little ones who haven't had chance to experience the effects of original sin. So don't blame yourself. Make a vow to treat Agnes better and confess your misdeeds to Father Lane next time you go to confession, and let's not mention it again. This little girl," she took the baby back and after kissing her cheek, laid her in her crib, "is in the hands of the Lord, so pray He doesn't want her back yet."

"I'll say Amen to that," replied her grandfather and Harriet repeated it.

142

A voice came from below. "Anybody home?"

"It's Missus Edwards from next door," exclaimed Harriet. "I'd better see what she wants," and she hurried out, but not before she saw the exchange of glances between her mother and grandfather.

Missus Edwards from next door was cuddling Tommy. "This one thought he'd been abandoned."

"We were only upstairs. Baby Winnie isn't well."

"I hope it isn't anything serious."

"We don't know." She had not actually asked what was wrong with the baby.

"Well, you know I'd take this one here off your hands if I could, but…"

"His mother's here now. I don't think she'd let you."

"I know, but the good news is my old man has found himself another job. It don't pay as well as the last one, but at least we won't lose the roof over our heads."

"That's wonderful. I'm pleased for him." She reached out to take Tommy. "Was there anything else? I mean, did you call round for…" Berating herself for being impolite, she stopped before she could offend the lady.

"No, I just came to see this little one." She kissed him and went through to the back. "It's snowing hard now, or I'd have offered to take him for a walk, although it's dark."

"Maybe another time, Missus Edwards. Thank you for calling." Harriet held the back door open whilst balancing Tommy on her skinny hip. He wriggled and she almost dropped him. "Good day," she called as she closed the door, feeling mean, but she could hear the hiss of the potatoes boiling over on the range.

Her grandfather joined her before she could do anything about it. "I'll see to that. You sit yourself down." He looked up at the clock. "I'm worried about Agnes. She should be back by now."

Her tongue between her teeth, to stop her making a hasty retort, Harriet sat Tommy on the carpet in the lounge.

The front door opened and his mother walked in, her face glowing. The coat she wore looked familiar. Had she been given permission to wear it?

Taking a deep breath, she counted to nine, not needing to reach ten, for the first few numbers calmed her. "Good day," she said in her most pleasant voice. "I trust you found it useful." What a load of drivel!

"Useful?" asked the girl as she hung the coat on the door.

Gampy greeted her. "I was becoming worried. How did it go?"

"Oh," Agnes looked from one to the other, "you mean jobwise?"

Harriet nodded. What else would they have meant?

Agnes warmed her hands in front of the fire. "Actually, I didn't find no job, but somefink much more exciting."

What could be more exciting than finding something with which to pay her way?

"I found me ma."

Harriet had not expected that. She tried to remember what the girl had told them about her family. "I didn't know you'd lost her," she tried to joke.

"Well, I 'adn't lost her." The girl obviously didn't have a sense of humour. "As I told yer she frew me out, but she says she's sorry."

"That's great news. So you'll be moving back in with her?" Harriet couldn't believe her luck. No longer would she have to put up with the usurper, although she must not call her that any more. Hadn't she vowed to treat the girl better?

However, her joy turned to ashes when Agnes replied, "Well, no, not x'acly."

Gampy put a finger in the works by adding, with a pointed look at Harriet, "You know you're welcome to stay here as long as you want. It's marvellous news that you've

144

made it up with your mother. Families shouldn't fall out. Life's too short for quarrels."

Chapter 19

The snow had fallen heavily during the night and Harriet thanked God for the new boots. Unable to make any speed, she slipped and slid, worried she would be late for work. Being Friday, payday, she would have to make it, come hell or high water, even if it meant breaking both her legs in the process.

Her pay had still not been agreed, so she daydreamed about all the things she could buy for Christmas presents if her grandfather didn't want it all: a pair of slippers for her ma, and a rattle for Tommy, although, with a bit of luck, he and his mother might have left by then. Missus Bowe had not given her the bootees she'd offered to knit for the twins, but she knew they'd be ready in time. What about Miss Louisa, though?

She pulled up, almost sliding on a particularly icy patch, and grabbed a shop window sill. What could she buy her? That particular shop sold beautiful parasols, but would she be able to afford one? Peering through the frosty glass, she tried to make out the price, but surely it couldn't be that much? The handle was made of bone or some such material. Would Miss Louisa like it? She'd never find out, for the price was way out of her range.

Miss Louisa met her as snow fell once more.

Harriet thanked her again for the boots, adding, "I'd have wet feet in my old ones."

"You are very welcome, my dear. I had wondered if the leather might have cracked from being unused for so long."

"No, no, they're marvellous. I polished and polished them last night, 'cos Gampy said it'd keep them supple."

When her employer turned from hanging up her black velvet cloak, Harriet stroked its softness. It had silk lining and a high collar, with lace, encrusted with sequins, around the shoulders. How she would love to own something so plush, and what a good job only a few flakes of snow had fallen on it, or it would have been ruined. Fancy risking it in that weather. If she owned such a garment, she'd never go out in wet conditions. *But then I'd probably never wear the cloak at all,* she laughed to herself.

After another fondle, she went into the shop. Customers were already queuing outside the door, keeping them busy for over an hour.

One lady asked to look at a piece of black lace. "I need something to brighten it up," she said, tapping her teeth, her head to one side. "I know it's supposed to be mourning garb, but a little fancy work won't go amiss."

Remembering the cloak she had been examining earlier, Harriet fetched some black sequins from a drawer in one of the cupboards made from dark wood. "Would these be what you are looking for, madam?"

"How clever of you, my dear. They are perfect." The customer nodded vigorously. Harriet counted out as many as she required, pleased she'd used her initiative. Her grandfather was always telling her to use her loaf of bread, her head, and her new job gave her the opportunity to do so day in and day out. Had Miss Louisa noticed? No, she was busy serving another customer. Ah, well, she'd tell her later.

Her stomach cramped and she pressed it to ease the pain. Maybe her thoughts of the previous week had been correct? Could she be expecting a baby, or knapped as she had heard Missus Bowes say? Why else would her belly be swollen and hurting?

As soon as Miss Louisa had finished serving she blurted out, "Miss Louisa, I know I can ask you things I wouldn't ask Mama, although I have asked her before, but she's never given me an answer but...how do babies get into their mother's bellies?"

"Harriet, what a question to bother me with when I am so busy. Surely your mama would tell you, if you asked her again?"

"I have, many times, as I said, but she always palms me off."

Miss Louisa looked up from the book in which she'd been writing. "Why do you question me at this very moment? I… I have not told you anything about myself that I should not."

"No, no, it's me. I think I may be…" Her stomach griped again and she doubled over in pain.

"Ah, I see. Have your fairies visited you yet?"

She tried to stand up straight. "I don't know. Do fairies make babies?"

"No, my dear. If your fairies are present, it means the opposite."

"I don't understand. Heck, I need the lavvy." She ran out to the lavvy in the back yard, worried she had wet herself. However, when she checked her drawers, she covered her mouth to prevent herself from screaming. Blood! Were her innards falling out? Was that why she had such stomach ache? She tried to think what diseases made people bleed. Miss Louisa might sack her if she thought she had something she could pass on to the customers.

Her employer's voice filtered through the door. "Harriet? Is everything well, my dear?"

"I'm just coming, Miss Louisa. I just have a tummy upset." She daren't tell her the real reason she was taking so long.

"If it is your monthly blood flow, what we call fairies, here's something to mop it up."

How did she know about the blood? Did fairies always make people bleed?

The door opened a fraction and a hand appeared, containing a piece of cloth. "Put this in your knickers," Miss Louisa advised.

Not wanting to disobey, she took the cloth between her first finger and thumb, letting it dangle.

The voice had gone, so she assumed Miss Louisa had returned to the shop. What should she do? She needed to join her, or she would certainly be sacked. There was only so much sympathy an employer would have. With no other option, she stuffed the rag inside her drawers and ran into the kitchen to wash her hands, feeling filthy and defiled. Could she go into the shop? Surely all the customers would know? Would they be able to smell her?

"Damn the blinking fairies," she whispered as she dried her hands. "I'll no longer think of you as sweet, little, fluttering angels."

Miss Louisa winked at her. If that lady didn't mind her being in such a state, then why should anybody else? Busying herself, she kept as far a distance as was possible from the ladies she served, wishing the day would end so she could go home and lie down with a hot water bottle.

It seemed an age until five o'clock.

"How's the stomach?" asked Miss Louisa as she locked the door. "I remember when mine started. I was scared stiff that something awful had happened to me. In fact, I thought my innards were falling out."

"Oh, my days, that's exactly what I thought, but…"

"Did your mother not warn you?"

"I don't remember her saying anything about…" She dared not use the word 'blood'. It just seemed too dirty.

"You had better tell her when you arrive home, so she can find you some protection. Anyway, it seems appropriate that on the day you become a woman, you receive your first wage." Miss Louisa opened the till, counted money into her hand, and then took out another coin.

Harriet couldn't see what it was. Probably a penny, she thought, but soon forgot her inconvenience as excitement took over. How much would she receive?

149

Disappointment filled her when she saw what value coin her employer offered her. One penny. Was that all she had earned?

"This penny is for you, yourself, and, as you have worked so hard, and been such a help, I shall pay you one whole pound this week. Do not expect that much every week though." She gave her a handful of coins.

Harriet counted them. Indeed, a whole pound! She had not expected that much. "Oh, Miss Louisa." She hugged her as she jangled the money in her hand. "Thank you, thank you. I feel like the queen. Do you think she owns a whole pound?"

Miss Louisa laughed. "I'm sure she does, although I hear tell she never takes money when she goes out."

"I can buy Gampy a twist of tobacco, and you…"

Miss Louisa shook her head as she bagged the money from the till. "No, no, my dear, please do not go to the trouble of buying me anything. I have everything I need. Lancelot sees to that. You need this for yourself and your family. If you want to treat somebody, treat yourself. You've earned it."

"No," Harriet looked down at her feet, "I couldn't do that. I'll give it all to Gampy to pay the bills." She pictured his face when she turned up with such a fortune.

"Well, that's your choice. But I would like you to keep the penny."

She'd thought to give it to Missus Bowe for the bootees, so didn't reply. Hopefully she wouldn't want anything for knitting them.

Miss Louisa surprised her by asking, "Is your brother's fiancée still around? You haven't mentioned her today."

"Agnes? She was this morning. But I don't think she and William were engaged. They just…" What had they done? She had always believed one had to be married to have a baby. Why would nobody tell her how they were made? Who else could she ask? Old Mother Peele? The old

150

hag would know, but Harriet knew she wouldn't be brave enough to bother her with such questions.

The door locked behind them, she noticed one of the stars in the window had fallen down. Should she ask Miss Louisa to unlock the shop so she could reposition it? But her employer seemed in a hurry, looking around as if expecting someone. Nobody would notice until the morning. The light from the street lamp across the road only gave out a soft glow.

Mister Lighten appeared from across the road, puffing and panting.

"My dear, whatever is the matter?" asked Miss Louisa, clutching his sleeve. "You look coopered."

"My dear," he gasped, "I beg you not to use those common phrases." He bent over, to catch his breath.

Even when he could hardly draw breath, he had to scold his wife. Harriet sympathised with her.

"I am sorry, my dear. I shall rephrase that. You seem...what was that word I heard somebody say the other day? Knacked. Is that common?"

His arm raised and Harriet thought he was going to hit her. "Do not ever use that language. It is most inappropriate."

Harriet backed away, not wishing to be part of the argument. But what if he were to beat her, there in the street? As she stepped back, not heeding her position, her foot slipped off the kerb and, if it hadn't been for the speed of Mister Lighten catching her, she'd have fallen headlong onto the road.

"My dear!" Miss Louisa grabbed the back of her coat. "Did you hurt yourself?"

Harriet blinked as she straightened up. "I...I'm fine, thank you. I'd better be going home."

"If you are sure. Off you go. I shall see you in the morning."

With a backward glance, she was relieved to see the couple turn in the other direction, arm in arm, quarrel apparently forgotten. Had her thoughtless action saved her employer from a beating? It would have been worth it, although, the further she walked, the more her ankle ached.

On reaching Hare Street, however, the pain left her, as a dramatic scene unfolded in front of her. A child ran out of a house, screaming and bawling, waving her arms in the air. Before anybody could stop her, she ran into the road, where she fell under the hooves of a horse pulling a landau. Yanking on the reins, the carriage driver shouted to the horse to stop, but it bucked and careered across the road, into the path of another carriage which toppled over, spewing its passengers onto the cold, impacted snow.

Hampered by the sore ankle, Harriet hurried to the scene and gasped in horror at the girl she had befriended the previous week, lying still in the road, covered in blood.

"Frances, Frances," she cried, patting the girl's cheek. Her eyes remained closed.

A woman eased her away. "Do you know this girl?" she asked.

"Yes, she lives there with…" Harriet pointed to an old lady, presumably her grandmother, wrapped in a tatty shawl, standing at the door of the house. She stood up and hobbled to her.

Tears ran down the old lady's cheeks as she shook her head. "I shouldn't have shouted at her, but I didn't know she'd go running out like that."

Gampy hurried across. "Phew, Harriet, it wasn't you. Thank God. We heard the commotion."

"No, Gampy, it's Frances, the girl I told you about, who comes from the North. This is her grandmother." She couldn't introduce her because she didn't know her name, only Gramma Betty.

A man picked up the injured girl and carried her towards the house as Harriet took the lady's arm and steered her inside.

"Is she still alive?" asked the old lady as Harriet sat her in an armchair while the man laid Frances on the sofa.

"I hope so," replied Harriet, crossing her fingers behind her back, for the girl still hadn't opened her eyes.

The man who had carried her in asked, "Does she have any other relatives, besides the old lady?"

"She said her mother had come to live here, but I've never seen her." Harriet tried to remember what she had been told, and looked across at the grandmother for confirmation. The lady sat weeping into an old, tatty handkerchief, mumbling that it was all her fault.

Old Mother Peele rushed in and pushed the man to one side. "Let me see."

Everyone in the room held their breath as the sage examined the child. Harriet realised her fingers were still crossed, but kept them like that, not wanting to tempt providence, as she jiggled from one foot to the other.

A little hand crept into hers. She hadn't seen Isabel enter the room. With a gentle squeeze, she held it.

"Is she dead?" whispered her young friend.

Harriet tried to tell from Old Mother Peele's posture, but couldn't read her face. Eventually the sage straightened and turned to face the growing audience.

"Well?" asked one of the onlookers, impatient to know the diagnosis.

The old lady shook her head. Frances's grandmother screamed, and slumped further into her chair.

Everyone murmured until the sound of their voices became deafening, and Harriet wanted to escape, but Isobel clung to her.

"What did she say?" cried the child. "Is Frances dead?"

Not wanting to be the one to give her the bad news, Harriet looked for Missus Leekes, but there was no sign of her in the crush surging forward to see for themselves. "Let's find your ma," she told her as she steered a path through.

Isobel had other plans. "But I want to see my friend."

"That's not a good idea. Come on, let's take you home."

"No." The child stamped her foot.

Harriet couldn't drag her away, so she let her go. Her grandfather held out his arms, and she gratefully fell into them, crying, "I saw her run out, but I couldn't stop her."

"It wasn't your fault, child. Don't distress yourself with needless guilt," he tried to console her, but she felt responsible. He led her outside into the increasing chaos.

One man attempted to direct the traffic around the upturned carriage, but riders, too impatient to wait, tried to squeeze through on the inside, causing more casualties.

"Come away, child," Gampy steered her towards number four, where her mother stood in the doorway, shivering, with only a thin shawl around her shoulders.

Forgetting her injured ankle, Harriet tripped as she ran between two horses.

Gampy caught her. "What's the matter, child? Are you trying to commit suicide?"

"I forgot I hurt my ankle earlier."

He helped her across, his arm around her waist and her mother stood aside for her to pass. "What's happening out there?" she asked. "I couldn't sleep with all the brouhaha."

After she and her grandfather had filled her in on the situation, Harriet could hear Tommy gurgling in his pram, and a faint mewling sound from one of the twins upstairs. Most of the noise from the street had been shut out with the closing of the front door, and her nerves calmed as she dropped into a chair.

"Where's Agnes?" asked her mother, poking a coal back into the fire.

"Who cares?" she mumbled, hoping not to have been heard, but clearly she had, judging by the glare her grandfather gave her.

"She went outside earlier," he replied, glancing through the doorway. "I'll look for her and check if there's anything I can do out there."

"Pa, there's enough folk out there," argued her mother, sitting down. "Put the kettle on for a brew, there's a dear."

Gampy nodded. "Yes, a good idea. I could make everyone a good, strong cup of rosie lee."

"I meant for us," answered her mother.

"Of course. I'll make you one first, but then I'll do my duty and help those outside." He went through to the kitchen.

"I ought to do that," protested Harriet, although not moving.

With an outstretched hand, her mother made as if to stop her. "No, dearie, let him be. He likes to feel useful."

Needing no further bidding, she leant back and closed her eyes, but her ankle throbbed, so she decided to take off her boot. Her fingers shook when she tried to unlace it. The incident outside had had more effect on her than she'd realised.

Gampy placed their drinks on a table and lifted her foot. "Let me. My, my, it is swollen. However did you walk all the way home like this?" he exclaimed when he eventually pulled off the boot.

"It wasn't as bad then," she replied as a knock on the door made them all turn.

Her grandfather opened it. "It's a policeman."

Her mother pulled a blanket over her to hide her nightclothes, but he averted his eyes and looked directly at Harriet. "I understand you witnessed the accident, Miss Harding." He took off his helmet and looked around as if to find somewhere to put it, but tucked it under his arm and took out a notebook and pencil.

She looked at her grandfather for moral support. Was the man going to arrest her?

"Don't look so worried. I need to know the facts."

She told him everything she'd seen. "I'm sorry it isn't much. Is Frances dead?"

Shaking his head, he closed his book and eyed the cup on the table. "No, no, they've taken her to the hospital."

Harriet breathed a sigh of relief. "Thank goodness for that."

"That's wonderful news." Gampy offered him the drink. "You must be ready for one of these."

The policeman's face lit up. He drank it in one go and handed the cup to Harriet, who gritted her teeth. That had been hers. Maybe Gampy would make her another, but he accompanied the constable outside, talking to him about all and sundry, not caring about her at all.

"I suppose I'll have to make it," she grumbled and turned to her mother. "Would you like a top-up?"

"No, thank you, dearie. I'd better feed the twins. Would you entertain Tommy 'til Agnes returns?"

She didn't reply as she shuffled towards the kitchen. He had better not need picking up, for she wouldn't be able to support him. Her stomach cramped and she remembered what had happened earlier that day. Should she bother her mama? But the rag Miss Louisa had given her felt sodden, so she'd need a new one. Had she anything in her drawer she could rip up? An old vest or petticoat? But her mama would find it and want to know what had happened to it. *Take the plunge, and tell her.* "Mama," she called as her mother was halfway up the stairs.

"Yes, dearie?"

"I…um…" How could she phrase it? "You know fairies?"

"Fairies?" A light seemed to dawn in her head. "Oh, your fairies? Have you…?"

She nodded.

"Then follow me and I'll find you some rags. I wondered when it would happen. You're already older than I was when mine started."

She hobbled up the stairs after her mother and they rifled through the drawers. "There aren't many left. I had to give Agnes some yesterday," said her mother. "Don't you have an old petticoat? I seem to remember one had a few holes. It must be too small for you by now. You can cut that into strips."

That had been her idea earlier. She should have done that anyway.

The scissors were downstairs in the sewing basket, so she found the item of clothing and took it down to find baby Tommy trying to climb out of the pram. "How long have you been able to pull yourself up like that, young man?" she exclaimed as she grabbed him. "We'll have to tie you in, in future. Or, at least, your mother will need to take more care. Why isn't she here to look after you?" A niggling thought told her that maybe the girl in question was outside, tending to the injured. Well, she should be looking after her son. She placed him on the floor with a rattle.

As she cut the white strips of material she wondered how she'd be able to walk to the shop the following morning if her ankle hadn't recovered. She couldn't afford to stay away and, anyway, she was enjoying her work. Her wages! How could she have forgotten them? She jumped up, hopped over to her coat on the back of the door, and felt in her pocket. No, she must have put it in the other one. But that was also empty. *Think! Where else could you have put it?* It wasn't as if it had been a single coin. One could have fallen out, but that many? She racked her brain, trying to recall in detail. Miss Louisa had given her the money—two shillings, four half-crowns, four florins, and, of course, the penny—and she had rolled them around with delight, never having owned so much before. Then what? Had she put them down while she put on her coat? Had her coat already been on? No, she definitely remembered being paid as soon as the door had closed on the last customer. But did she have it when she witnessed the accident? She recalled turning the coins over in her pocket. All the way home, in fact, and she had even taken some out and surreptitiously looked at them, making sure no pickpockets had been about to steal them. Oh, no! Had she been too obvious? Had one sidled up beside her and slipped his hand in her pocket while her attention had been focused on the accident?

Tears fell down her cheeks as she slumped onto the sofa. How could she have been so stupid? What would Gampy say? They might even have to move out if he couldn't pay the bills.

She started as the door opened and he came in, wiping his brow. "Phew, what a movver and farver—a palaver. I never saw such mayhem, bodies and blood everywhere."

Too wound up to reply, she grimaced. Her face felt like a gargoyle on a church wall, ugly and distorted.

He didn't appear to notice as he recounted the details of the scene outside and picked up Tommy. "It's just as well you didn't see any of it, young sir," he crooned to the baby, and then turned back to Harriet. "Is your mother still upstairs?"

She nodded, still too anxious to speak.

"What's the matter, girl? Is it your ankle?" That had completely slipped her mind. Should she pretend that was her problem? But it paid to be honest, so she was always told. "No, it's..."

But she was spared when he put Tommy down and fished into his pocket. "By the way, I found this on the floor earlier when you were talking to that policeman. I assume it's yours." He held out a handful of coins. Her wages.

"On the floor? How...? Puzzled, she put out her hand to take them. "I don't understand."

"Your coat fell off the hook and they must have fallen out."

"How did I not notice?"

He shrugged. "You were wrapped up giving your account of the accident, and clearly paid no heed to what I was doing."

"My word, Gampy, I wish you'd told me earlier. I've been frantic, thinking some dipper had pinched it on my way home, and that we'd have to go to that awful workhouse."

He put his arm around her. "You soft ha'porth. Even without your wages things wouldn't be that dire. I have money. Mind you, it won't last long if you go around losing yours." He ruffled her hair. "Anyway, we'd better get some mortal sinner cooked, or we'll all starve to death."

Thanking God, she hugged him and held out the money. "Please may I keep a little of it to buy Christmas presents?"

He closed her hand around it. "You keep it all, child. We'll manage."

"No, I can't do that. Gampy, please take it. I want to pay my way. That's why I found the job."

"Just this once you may have it all. Start paying me next week."

But if her ankle still throbbed the following day she'd not make it to the shop, so would have no wages. "I'm so pleased Frances isn't dead," she said as she counted the coins once more to make sure they were all there. When he nodded, she sighed. "I wish I could've stopped her, but she just ran out."

"Don't blame yourself, my girl. Here, peel these squawky parrots, would you?" He washed a carrot and handed it to Tommy to chew on while the dinner cooked.

"But what shall I do with this money? Where shall I keep it? I've never seen so much before. Well, maybe, once, when Mama asked me to pay Missus Green's bill, but that doesn't count, 'cos it weren't mine."

"Don't you have a goldilocks?"

"A what?"

"A money box?"

"It's upstairs, in my…I mean your…bedroom. It has a farthing in that I've been saving for a rainy day. These beauties can join it. I'll take them up later." She put the coins behind a jar of pickle on the shelf and picked up a carrot. Her eyes kept being drawn to them, as if by a magnet, and every now and again she touched them, to make sure they were real.

"They won't disappear, girlie." Her grandfather grinned. "I remember my first pay about tuppence halfpenny, or some such trifling amount. To me it was a fortune." He stared into space, casting his mind back. "I ran away to sea, you know, without telling Ma what I intended."

"She must have been worried sick." As if she hadn't heard the story many a time, she liked to play along with him. She never tired of it.

"Yes, but I never realised at the time. Thirteen, I was, well, almost. Thought I knew it all. The world…" With a deep breath, he came round from a trance. "But this won't cook the dinner. Chop, chop, lass, is that your mother knocking on the ceiling?" He doubled over, laughing. "Well, obviously not on the ceiling. She'll be banging on the floor, not the ceiling."

When Harriet looked at him askance, he knocked her arm, almost pushing her over. She landed on her bad ankle, which she had been trying to keep off the floor, and yelped.

"My child, I'm so sorry. I forgot all about your bad leg." He steered her towards a chair and sat her down. "You can do your chores from there."

The carrots finished and dropped into the pot as her grandfather went upstairs to see what her mother had wanted, she hobbled over to the dresser and picked up her

160

money again and dropped it in her pocket, enjoying the chink as they landed. Agnes should be in soon. Not that she didn't trust her. But as her pa had often told her, 'Don't leave temptation in anyone's path'.

"Oh, Papa, why did you die? I…we need you."

Her grandfather came down and glanced around. "Who were you talking to? I thought Agnes must have returned."

"No, Gampy, she hasn't." Why did his first thought have to be about the tart? Her eyes widened and she gasped, hoping he hadn't heard her thoughts, but he'd obviously forgotten what he'd asked, since he'd satisfied himself his new favourite girl wasn't there, and opened the front door. A chilly blast blew in.

"Brr, it's freezing," he exclaimed as he closed it again. "The chaos seems to have died down. The traffic's moving freely, so Agnes should be in any minute. I was hoping to tell her dinner was almost ready, but there's no sign of her."

Harriet shook her head and whispered to Tommy, "Your ma has taken over your great-grandfather's heart, I fear." His face screwed up and he bawled. "No, don't do that," she cried. "I didn't mean it in an insulting way. I was just being a misery guts. Please don't cry."

She put him down, flinching at the pain in her ankle.

"Is that clothes peg still giving you grief?" Gampy surprised her by asking. Perhaps he did still love her.

"Yes, Gampy. It hurts like Hell. Sorry, I mean a lot. How on earth will I walk to work tomorrow?"

"Um, that's what your ma's concerned about too. But I've been thinking; maybe there's someone who could take you? Do we know anyone with a carriage?"

Harriet spluttered. "Gampy, as if."

"Um, well, a horse and cart, then."

"There aren't many of them around these parts. If we lived on a farm, maybe, like some of the people you tell me stories about."

He stroked his beard and sucked in his lips, then his eyes lit up as he suggested, "Agnes and I could support either side of you and be your human splints. Now, that's a good idea."

She opened her mouth to refute the proposal, but closed it again, saying eventually, "I don't think she'd be willing."

"Why not? She seems a very helpful type of girl to me. I don't know why you don't like her." Gampy stalked off into the kitchen and Harriet could hear him stirring the gravy in the saucepan.

She followed him and rested her forehead on his bent back. "I'm sorry, Gampy. You're only trying to help, and all I do is put a damper on every suggestion you make. I'm acting like a spoilt brat, and I had determined to change, but…"

"It'll be the shock of what's happened out there." With arms outstretched, he enfolded her. "Everything will work out to the good. Trust me. You listen to your old Gampy."

With a nod, she pulled away as something tugged at her dress. A gasp escaped her as she looked down. "Tommy, how did you get there?" she exclaimed, picking him up and handing him to her grandfather. "He must have crawled. I didn't know he could do that."

"No, me neither. We'll have to keep a close watch on him in future. We can't leave him sitting playing any more. And there was me thinking we could borrow his jar of jam and wheel you to work in it."

"Oh, Gampy, you're funny." Her face creased into a grin as she imagined herself lying in the perambulator with a bottle of milk stuck in her mouth.

He ruffled her hair, looking worried. "Where on earth can Agnes be?"

Chapter 20

When Agnes still hadn't returned by the time dinner was ready, Gampy put on his coat and opened the door. "I'm going to find her."

"But your dinner will get cold," protested Harriet.

"Hers'll be even colder. I'm worried now."

"Shall we start, Mama?" asked Harriet after he had gone. "Or do you think I ought to go after him?"

Her mother sighed. "I don't know, dearie. Yes, we may as well. He'll be back any minute. There's no point in all of us having cold food." She put a potato in her mouth but, before they had eaten another mouthful, the door burst open and Gampy ran in. "She's hurt. The carriage that turned over fell on her."

"My word," exclaimed Harriet. "Hurt badly?"

A man appeared, carrying a blood-stained Agnes.

Harriet jumped up to clear the sofa so he could lay her on it, while her mother ran to the kitchen and filled a bowl with water.

"I'm all right," moaned Agnes.

"You don't look it," said Harriet, grabbing the flannel from her mother, and wiping off the blood. Was it her fault the girl had been injured? If she had treated her better...

Gampy stood biting his fingers. "Why didn't I see you earlier? I was out there for a long while. But I never thought to search among the wounded."

"Don't blame yourself, Gampy," said Harriet. "It's more likely to be my fault than yours."

"It ain't nobody's fault," retorted Agnes, trying to sit up. "I were just unlucky."

"But how did you happen to be there just at that moment?" asked Gampy.

"You was asleep on the sofa and Missus was upstairs, so I fought I'd meet 'Arriet from work. I were goin' to take Will…I mean, Tommy, but 'e were asleep too, so it seemed better to leave 'im. When I only got a few yards up the street, suddenly all 'ell broke loose, and then everything went black."

So it was my fault, thought Harriet.

"Have you broken any bones?" asked her mother.

"Don't fink so." Agnes shook her legs and arms. "Just me 'ead."

"Let me look." She examined her. "I wonder if we ought to ask Mother Peele to…"

"No, Missus. Please, I just want ter sleep."

Harriet moved aside as her mother covered the girl with a blanket.

***

Snow lay in drifts across the street as Harriet drew back the front room curtains. Apart from a few foolhardy riders, nothing much moved outside, and she couldn't make out where the pavement ended and the road began. The front doors of the houses opposite were covered as high as the handles. Was theirs as bad? Twisting her neck, she tried to look through the side of the window, but couldn't make it out. As she opened the door a tiny space, a voice called from behind, making her jump, and she pulled it more than she had intended, bringing a pile of snow inside. With all her might, she pushed the door closed, but what should she do with the mound of white stuff on the frayed carpet? "Look what you made me do," she cried.

"We'll make tea with it," replied her grandfather. "You can't beat a cuppa made with melted snow."

"But it'll be dirty."

He ran his fingers through it. "It'll do. Quick, before it melts."

She hurried to pick up a pan and they scooped as much as they could into it with their hands. "I'll fetch a spoon for the rest," she called as she went once more to the kitchen, noticing that Tommy had awoken, probably by their voices. Should she take him out? But he would only crawl in the wet patch and catch cold. The fire hadn't yet been lit, so he'd have no means of warming up.

The dampness mopped with an old towel, she moaned, "I'll never reach the shop. Even though my ankle seems slightly better today, it'd take me hours in this weather."

"No, girlie. But light the fire. We'll all die from chills, otherwise." He picked up Tommy.

The simple task didn't take long, so she banked it up, and soon flickering flames raced each other up the chimney. The coal scuttle had been emptied in her efforts, but she didn't fancy going to the outhouse to fill it. The back door might be covered as much as the front one. But needs must. Agnes hadn't seemed too worse for wear by bedtime, but hadn't put in an appearance, and she couldn't expect her mother to leave her bed and do it, so that left one person. Herself.

Her grandfather still sat playing with Tommy. Maybe, if she hinted enough, he would fetch it. "Is there plenty of coal left?" she asked.

"We're low, but there should be enough for a few days. I hope this snow doesn't linger or we'll all wind and breeze."

He hadn't taken the hint, merely continued crooning to the baby, so she had no option but to go herself. "Right, I'll go outside in the cold snow and fetch some."

"Good girl."

An old tattered coat hung on a peg on the back door; she pulled it over her shoulders and picked up the scuttle. "I'll go now, then."

A quick glance told her he wasn't going to budge, so she opened the door, just a fraction at first, then, when no snow fell in, drew it further back. "I can't go out there, Gampy," she yelled, pushing the door to once more. "It's about six feet deep. I'll get lost, and you'll find my frozen body, curled up in a ball, in a week's time."

"Don't be so daft. When I was your age I had to walk three miles to school and back in deeper snow than that."

"But you said you left school at twelve or thirteen. I'm nearly fourteen."

Gampy stood up. "You know what I mean. Anyway, I'd better make this youngster some breakfast." As he handed Tommy to her, a grimace covered his face.

"Are you well, Gampy?" she exclaimed with a frown. "You look in pain."

"I'm fine, girlie. All goosey and gandy. Do we have any porridge oats left?"

With another glance at his white face, she took the jar from the pantry. "Are you sure?"

"Yes, girl, I told you. Stop twittering. Seeing as you're unwilling, I'll shovel the back yard. We need to reach the lavvy and the coal, which is probably more important."

"Gampy, I'll do it."

"No, child. I'm the man of the house. It's my job."

With a shake of the head, she handed him the coat, but he brushed it aside. Used to rough elements, he didn't often wear such a garment. But he wasn't young any more. She shrugged, knowing there was no point trying to urge him to do something he didn't want.

The sound of the shovel scraping against the hard ground must have awakened Agnes, for she came in, yawning. "Gor blimey, it's cold," she exclaimed, drawing her hand across her mouth and yawning again.

"How are you this morning?" Harriet asked, peering at her cuts and bruises.

"All right. We've had a fair fall o' snow, ain't we?"

"Yes, we have, and Gampy's out there, clearing a path. Some of us have been up ages, seeing to your son and warming the house."

"Fanks. You should've woke me."

You shouldn't need waking, Harriet wanted to say but bit her tongue, repeating her vow to treat the girl more kindly, especially in the light of her experience the day before. "Anyway, I need a plan of how to get to work."

"Will the shop be open today?"

"Maybe not. But I ought to go, in case. Miss Louisa lives close by, so she mightn't have difficulty making her way there."

"But what about your bad ankle?" Agnes shifted Tommy to her other knee so she could examine it. She seemed genuinely concerned. "She wouldn't expect you to hobble all that way in these conditions."

"She doesn't know I hurt it."

A clash and a thump startled them. Harriet ran to the back door to see her grandfather on his knees, trying to stand. With her hand under his arm she yelled, "I knew I shouldn't have let you do it. You're too old."

"Don't you...call me...old," he stuttered as he gained his foothold. "I merely slipped."

"You didn't get that pain again, did you?"

He didn't reply and, after helping him indoors, she went out to finish the job. Sweat ran down her back before she had made much headway, and her ankle throbbed. Should she suggest Agnes take over? She had a good excuse, though, being hurt in the accident, and Gampy would only berate her, so she dug and dug. Clouds of her breath could be seen in the still, cold air, and, as she stopped to wipe her brow she noticed white flakes fluttering down. Oh, no, not more snow! The first lot had not cleared. With renewed vigour, she shovelled once more. They had to have coal.

Agnes came out as she reached the coalhouse door. "Well done. Drink?"

"That would be lovely," she said in her sweetest voice. "But first, help me open this damned door." A glimmer of surprise showed on the girl's face at the profanity, but between them, they managed to yank it open. "Now, please fetch the scuttle so I may fill it."

"'Course. You look done in. You should've asked me to 'elp," replied Agnes as she scooted off, leaving Harriet chuntering under her breath.

Back inside, her hands around a welcome mug of tea, she examined her grandfather's face while his attention was diverted by Tommy, who had not been dressed, so could not understand why his long nightshirt kept wrapping around his legs as he tried to crawl.

As she opened her mouth to rebuke Agnes for not dressing him, the other girl stunned her by proclaiming that she had no clean clothes for him. *I'm not doing your washing, so you needn't think I'm offering, even if you have had an accident.*

Her grandfather remained staring at the baby. He didn't look at all well. "Gampy, are you sure you're all right?" she asked, putting her hand on his shoulder.

"Just a bit hell-fired, my dear, nothing to worry about," he replied with a half smile.

"No wonder you're tired, sleeping on that hard..." Her finger indicated towards the front room and she gave Agnes a pointed look.

"It's not that. I've slept in more uncomfortable places at sea. Did I tell you about the time we almost hit an iceberg, off the coast of Alaska?" His face became more animated as he recounted the story she had heard many times before, but, of course Agnes hadn't. The other girl sat spellbound as he recounted the tale, with additions, to make it even more dramatic.

As he told his story Harriet peeped out of the window. It had stopped snowing, but what about work? In answer to her thoughts, a knock came on the front door. But if she opened it, they would be inundated by snow again. A scraping noise meant the visitor must be clearing it away. She opened the letter box to peep through, to see who it might be. "Good day, sir," she called to the brown trousers, the only part of the visitor she could see.

"Miss Harding?" the young man bent down and called.

"Yes, sir, please wait while I open the door." Fancy conducting a conversation through a letter box! The door creaked as she pulled it, and her eyes opened wide when she saw the caller's face. The young man from church with the beautiful blue eyes. What was he doing on her doorstep? And how did he know her address, or her name, for that matter?

"Miss Harriet Harding?" he repeated, smiling at her astonished face.

"Yes, but…"

"Don't worry."

Believe me, sir, I'm not worried.

"Mistress Little sent me."

"Pray, come in." With trembling hands, she knocked away the pile of snow he hadn't cleared, and opened the door. "Pray, excuse the mess." Dirty baby clothes and paraphernalia littered the floor and she grabbed a handful and hid it under a cushion, indicating for him to sit, but he remained standing, a frown on his face, as he took off his hat.

Agnes came through with Tommy, who was crying, a most unusual occurrence.

"Ah," he exclaimed, turning to Harriet. "The baby isn't yours, then?"

"What? No, of course not. I…" Why would he even consider such a preposterous suggestion? "No, he's my brother's, my dead brother's. This is his… This is Agnes, the baby's mother. And that gentleman there is my grandfather. I'm sorry, but I don't know your name." At last, she would find out.

"Benjamin. Benjamin Toghill." He bowed.

"How have you managed to come all this way, Mister Toghill? I mean, in such awful conditions." *Keep calm,* she told herself, but her heart beat ten to the dozen, and he must have heard it.

"I am very resilient. Mistress Little happened to see me near the shop, and she seemed concerned, so I asked if I could help. In reply, she asked me if I would be so kind as to inform you that she will not be opening today." He stood twiddling his hat.

"Pray, sir, do sit down. You've come all this way. Let me offer you a drink. Tea?" Should she ask if he wanted something stronger? Her father might have left some brandy.

Her grandfather saved her the bother. "I think the young man deserves something stronger than tea, my dear." He opened the bottom cupboard in the sideboard, took out an almost full bottle of rum, and showed it to the man. "You can't beat a drop of rum. I remember when I was on board ship, it warmed me through like nothing else." He grabbed two glasses and half-filled them, before giving Mister Toghill a shove into the armchair, and related another tale.

Harriet turned away, trying to smother a grin, as the young man listened attentively to the old tar, occasionally taking a small sip of drink. From the grimace he made at the first taste, Harriet could tell he didn't like it. He had probably never tasted it before, but was too polite to refuse.

At least she didn't have to worry about going to work. But what could she say to Benjamin—she whispered his name to herself as she went out to fill the coal scuttle— once her grandfather had finished his story? However much she didn't want him to leave, she couldn't keep him there indefinitely.

As she carried the scuttle inside, he jumped up, almost spilling what remained in his glass. "Miss Harding, allow me." He grabbed it from her, and chucked coal onto the fire. It had not needed mending and she feared the huge flames would set the chimney on fire. "Dear, oh, dear," he muttered. "Maybe I should not have done that." With the tongs, he lifted off a few cobbles.

"Please, sir, do not concern yourself." She took the tongs from him and doing so, caught his gaze. What a beautiful sight. Such blue eyes. Mesmerised, she froze, the utensils in mid air. He made no move to stir either.

Her grandfather coughed behind them. "What did you say your name was, again, young sir?"

"Benjamin Toghill, sir," he replied, blinking, as if coming round from a trance. "Pray, excuse me, I must be going."

"No, no, young man, stay a while. Are you related to the Toghills of Brick Lane?" Receiving a muffled reply of, "No, sir, not that I know of," he continued, "Look, it's snowing hard again. Take off your coat." Gampy started to undo the buttons and once they had been unfastened, he pulled the coat off the young man's shoulders and hung it on the door, ignoring any protestations to the contrary.

"Gampy," hissed Harriet.

"Shush, child. It would be very imprudent for the young sir to venture out in such conditions."

With raised eyebrows, Harriet shook her head in apology. She had no intention of imploring him to stay. He might have other errands to run, more important than her silent wishes. Should she say anything about church? He hadn't admitted to seeing her before and, maybe, didn't recognise her. Never mind. If they managed to go the following day, she would speak to him, knowing they had been introduced.

A shriek from upstairs alerted them all. Agnes had been playing in the kitchen with Tommy, and she and Harriet arrived at the stairs at the same time. Harriet shoved her out of the way and ran up, two at a time, praying, "Please, God, don't let it be Winifred."

171

Her mother lay on the floor, crying.

"Is it the baby?" Harriet raced over to look at the twins, but they both seemed to be sleeping peacefully. She touched them, just to make sure, and they felt warm. "What's the matter, then?" When her mother did not reply, she glanced up at the spot on the ceiling. Could her father have done something to make her mother such a quivering wreck?

"I'm sorry, dearie." Her mother stood up, as Agnes and Gampy came into the bedroom. "I was having a nightmare, and fell out of bed, imagining dragons and monsters climbing all over me. I'm so sorry to have worried you."

Relieved, Harriet helped her into bed. "Thank goodness it was only that, Mama. How's Winnie today?"

"See for yourself. She's much recovered, thank God. I may come downstairs in a little while. I've stayed up here too long." She pulled the blankets over her and snuggled into them. "I'll just have another five minutes."

They trooped out and Harriet remembered their guest. Had he been left alone? She found him dangling Tommy on his knee, singing a little ditty.

"My papa used to sing that to me, when I was a little girl," she exclaimed. "Gallopy trots, gallopy trots, gallopy, gallopy, gallopy…trots. How I used to love it when he dropped me between his knees at the last word. But how do you know it, sir?"

"I have several nieces and nephews, and the younger ones love the game. It was also one of my favourites."

"Ah, they must be the ones I see with you and your family at church occasionally?"

He nodded.

So he had recognised her. "Your mother came into the shop the other day."

"Yes, she told me."

"Really? She didn't acknowledge me. I didn't even think she'd recognised me."

An abashed face stared at her. "Actually, that was the reason I was hanging around there this morning."

"What, to see your mother?"

He laughed. "No, to catch a glimpse of you."

Her face reddened as she caught her breath.

Agnes took Tommy, leaving Benjamin—as she thought of him—to walk over to take his coat off the door.

"You aren't going, are you? I mean, you've just…"

"Yes, I fear I must. You have reminded me my mother asked me to buy some groceries."

What a thoughtful son. "Missus Green on the corner sells very good produce."

"Yes, I know. My mother often patronises her establishment." He put on his coat as Agnes pulled a face at her behind his back, evidently unused to hearing such refined language. Harriet ignored her as thoughts ran through her brain of how to prolong their meeting. "We need some…um…don't we, Gampy? I could accompany the gentleman."

Her grandfather looked askance at her.

"Porridge, that's what we're almost out of—porridge." She grabbed her coat, pushing to the back of her mind the fact that she shouldn't be going anywhere with the man, unaccompanied. But what could happen on such a snowy street? "We cannot manage without porridge, and Mister Toghill would be my protection from the dippers and blaggards who may be lurking in the alleyways."

Gampy's eyes raised and Agnes snorted. She glared at the girl, adding, "That is of course, as long as the gentleman does not mind escorting me."

"No, no, not at all. I would be delighted."

She stuck out her tongue at Agnes and, with another glare, opened the door, catching her breath at the freezing waft of air that blew in.

"Mind your ankle, girlie," called her grandfather. "You don't want to be hurting that."

The pain had almost been forgotten in the excitement of meeting her heart-throb in person. A brave face was required. She could not allow him to support her. But then again…

"Maybe I need a warm shawl," she muttered as she grabbed one from the back of the sofa and wrapped it around her head. Not wanting to keep her young man waiting, she raced out.

He stamped his feet. "Brr, it's colder than ever. Are you sure you want to venture out? Especially if you have a bad leg."

"It's nothing." Her teeth gritted as she realised it hurt more than ever, she tried not to limp. Should she hold his arm? Would it be proper? Her friend, Lucy, waved from her window as they passed. She raised her head, not enough to look snooty, though, and carried on, giving a small gesture of acknowledgement as she fished into her coat pockets to see if she had left her gloves inside. Yes, what luck.

The gloves pulled on, she passed the house of Frances's grandmother. The door opened and the girl herself came out with a lady Harriet assumed was her mother.

"How lovely to see you, Frances. I'm so glad you're recovered," she said, nodding to the lady.

"Yes. Me mam's taking me to buy a lollipop."

"That's nice."

They walked in the opposite direction, leaving Harriet to wonder why the girl should have a treat after behaving so badly.

"Is your mother unwell?" Benjamin surprised her by asking as they continued towards the shop.

"I…um, not unwell as such. She's just had twin babies, and is still lying in."

"I see. I apologise for being a nosey parker. I should not have asked."

"That's fine. We don't stand on ceremony in our house." The words came out without thought and she sounded as if they didn't care how they acted. From his well-heeled accent, it seemed he came from a well-to-do family, and might look down on hers. "I mean..." How could she put things right?

"No more do we," he replied, setting her fears at rest.

"Do you have brothers and...? Yes, of course you do. You've already told me you have nieces and nephews. But are you the only one still at home?" Her babbling tongue would be her downfall one day. Why did she not think before she opened her mouth?

Not taking enough notice of where she was walking, she almost bumped into a lamppost, and Benjamin grabbed her, pulling her against his hard body. "I...um...oh..." She could barely breathe for the impact, or was it the reaction to his closeness?

"You need to watch your step," he rebuked her, but as she looked up, she saw him smile.

"Yes, I do," she replied, pulling slightly away. "You're my knight in shining armour."

His chuckle echoed along the deserted street. Frances and her mother had disappeared. Only the occasional rider on horseback dared to face the elements, no carriages, and the only other living thing was a mangy black dog, trying to paw at something in the gutter.

"I hope the shop's open," she exclaimed as they continued on their way. "It should be, for Missus Green lives in the back, so she won't have to go out to get there, if you know what I mean?" *There I go again, babbling.*

He peered through the snow that was falling once more. "I can see a light in the window, so it looks like it."

"Thank goodness for that. I should hate to have brought you on a wild goose chase."

"I was coming anyway, remember."

"Yes, of course." She blew out her cheeks. Why couldn't she speak with any intelligence? Had her brain become addled by the cold weather?

They arrived at the shop, surprised to see it full of customers. When had they arrived? She had not seen anybody go in while they were walking towards it.

"You go first, Miss Harding." Benjamin ushered her towards the counter, once their turn came.

"Thank you." What had she come for? Porridge, oh yes. She placed her order, and then slapped her forehead with her hand, for she had not brought any money. Fiddlesticks. Dare she ask for the item to be put on the bill? Had it been paid that week? Her grandfather hadn't mentioned it. They usually paid on a Friday but she'd been at work. What if she were refused? How embarrassing would that be, with Benjamin standing behind her?

"That'll be sixpence, if you please," demanded Missus Green.

Harriet raised her eyebrows and smiled at her, in the hope she would understand, but the lady stood, hands on hips, her mouth set in a severe line.

Trying to appear confident, she stated, "As usual, if you please, Missus Green."

The lady shook her head.

Oh, no, what could she do? "But I came out in such a rush I forgot my purse," she whispered.

"That don't help me. You knows the rules. Friday's the deadline."

Then the ultimate in humiliation happened, as Benjamin leaned forward and held out a shiny silver sixpence, saying, "Allow me." What else could she do but accept? Her head bent, she could have cried, but handed the coin to the grocer and stepped out of the way, clutching her purchase. They still had half a packet of the blooming stuff in the pantry. Why on earth had she thought of such a hare-brained idea?

About to leave without him, she thought better of it. She needed to repay him. He'd have to go back with her so she could run into the house and fetch the money.

Bowing to the customers who had entered after them, not daring to look anybody in the eye, she waited by the door while Benjamin collected his goods. One of the people might recognise her, and tell the whole street of her disgrace. She would be the laughing stock of the East End.

Eventually, Benjamin joined her, his goods in a brown bag. She raced out the door with him behind her. "Mister Toghill, I don't know how to thank you. We usually pay the bill each week, but what with Pa dying and the bad weather and Mama being laid up and everything, it must have been forgot. I've never been so shamed in my life. I..."

"Pray, do not distress yourself, my dear. It was a mere sixpence."

The amount was not what she was bothered about as much as being refused credit, and in front of him. How could he ever speak to her again?

"If you'd accompany me home, sir, I'll pay you straightaway. Please don't think this happens all the time."

He turned to face her. "My dear Miss Harriet, I would never consider such a thing. Do not upset yourself."

He'd called her by her name. That meant he mustn't be disturbed by the incident.

"We shall not speak of it ever again," he continued.

"So we will speak again, after today?"

"I certainly hope so. We are friends, now, are we not? How old are you, by the way?"

Should she lie? He seemed much older than she had previously thought. In church, he had seemed like a boy, but her opinion was now that he was a man. Her innate honesty overcame her qualms at him knowing she was a mere child, and she replied, "Almost fourteen, sir."

"Ah, slightly younger than I thought, but no matter."

"And you, sir, how old are you?" She bit her lip, wondering if she should have asked such an impertinent question.

"Almost nineteen."

"Ah, and do you have a job, sir? I mean…"

A figure loomed out of a shop doorway, making her step to one side. Benjamin grabbed her arm to prevent her stepping into the road just as a man on a horse rode by. Trust her to find the exact moment somebody was actually using the street. Not that she could differentiate between the edge of the pavement and the road itself, such was the depth of snow. She glanced up at her saviour, who was grinning. "Sir, I must thank you once again for rescuing me, in more than one sense of the word."

"My child, you are a walking hazard. You had better cling onto me for the remainder of the journey." He tucked her gloved hand under his arm, and she prayed he did not think she had done it on purpose, in order for him to do so.

A tinkly laugh came from her mouth. "Haha, sir, I'm not usually so clumsy." *Only when you're around,* she added, silently, as she gripped his arm. What bliss, touching his coat. Then she recalled the figure who had scared her, and turned around. Probably a vagrant. Many of them slept in doorways and such, too proud to go to the workhouse, until the police moved them on. "Don't you feel sorry for those wretched people?" she asked.

Benjamin stopped. "I beg your pardon?"

With her finger, she indicated the dark shape they had passed. "Those miserable men. Shouldn't we give him a farthing, or something?" Not that she had any money to give, but her escort seemed to have plenty.

He swivelled her around and marched off. "No, I do not. You beware of such as he. Miscreants, no-gooders, the lot of them."

"That isn't very Christian. Doesn't the priest say we should help our fellow men in distress?"

"Ah, is this your house?"

She had not been paying attention to their route, and pulled up sharply. "Yes, yes, of course, pray wait while I find the money I owe you." She opened the front door. "Or you could come in for a minute."

"No, thank you, my mother will be waiting for these." He lifted the bag of groceries. "Pay me next time you see me." He doffed his hat and made to walk away. "Good day."

She stared open-mouthed at his retreating back. Had she offended him? Had he taken offence at her calling him unchristian?

Her mother's voice called from inside the house, "Come in, dearie. You're letting out all the heat."

After one last glance up the road, she closed the door behind her, her mood dropping to the depths. Fifteen or so minutes before, she had been in heaven.

"Where did you scoot off to, in such a hurry?" her mother asked.

"Didn't Gampy tell you?" As she hung up her coat, she blew out her breath. "I...I've been making a fool of myself, Mama."

"Your grandfather said something about a young man. What did you think you were doing, going off like that, unescorted?"

Tears filled Harriet's eyes as she slumped onto the sofa. Her mother sat down and put her arm around her shoulders. "He hasn't abused you, has he? My dearie, your grandfather should have stopped you. I'll never forgive myself if..."

"No, Mama, no. He was exactly the opposite, very polite and genteel. In fact, he paid for the porridge." She pointed to the packet, lying on the windowsill where she had flung it.

"Porridge? What has that to do with anything?"

Harriet explained.

"Your grandfather should still have stopped you."

"I wish I hadn't gone. Anyway, where is Gampy? And Agnes, for that matter? Surely she isn't out looking a job in these conditions?"

"No, she's taken Tommy next door. Missus Edwards wanted to see him, and your grandfather nipped out for some baccy."

"I could have bought him some, to save him the bother. Why didn't he say?"

Her mother shrugged and stood up. "Anyway, I feel so much better today, so I think I'll dress, and brush my hair."

"How's baby Winnie? Is she still thriving?"

"Hopefully, but she still needs your prayers." Her mother started up the stairs but turned. "How's your foot, by the way?"

"Well, I had almost forgotten it, but it seems to be throbbing now." She took off her boot and examined it. "It's rather black and blue, but I'll live. What's the expression Gampy uses? Worse things have happened at sea."

"Good girl, that's the spirit."

"Would you like me to bring you a bowl of warm water, for a nice wash?" Harriet asked as she picked up the kettle.

"That'd be lovely, if it isn't too much trouble," came the reply as her mother continued up, singing softly, in her beautiful contralto voice.

Chapter 21

Dressed for church in her best clothes, Harriet hurried downstairs. Some of the snow had gone, but the street looked even more deserted than the day before. Nobody would be venturing out unless they had an urgent mission. And she had. She needed to ask Benjamin Toghill's forgiveness, if he was at Mass, of course.

Her grandfather sat up and yawned. "Where are you off to in such a flap and a flurry? It's barely nine o'clock. Mass isn't until ten."

"Are you coming, today, Gampy?" she asked. "Because I need to go early. I need to beg pardon from Ben...Mister Toghill, for offending him yesterday. I've hardly slept all night, worrying that he might never speak to me again."

"Ah, young love." Her grandfather yawned again, and scratched his bald head. "I might give it a miss today, what with the snow and everything."

"You're not poorly, are you, Gampy?" She sat beside him, staring into his face, and stroking his white beard. "You would tell me if you were, wouldn't you?"

He turned away. "Of course I'm not, girlie. I'm all...tell us a story, whig and tory, hunky dory. Don't you go worrying about me. Make us a cup of rosie lee, would you?"

"If you're sure."

He nudged her off the sofa as noises came from upstairs. "Agnes said she might go to church," he called as she went into the kitchen.

In amazement, she poked her head round the doorway. "Agnes? Church? But she's committed a mortal sin, hasn't she? Having a baby without being married?"

"We all make mistakes, and if we beg exculpatation, and promise not to commit the sin ever again, God forgives us if we're sorry."

"Excul...what? Is that another of your rhyming words, Gampy," she laughed. "'Cos I can't think of what it rhymes with."

He laughed, also. "No, it's a proper word. Is that tea mashed? A person could die from thirst in this house."

As she poured out his tea—she was only allowed water before Holy Communion—she pondered on his words. Did God really forgive every sin? Had she committed one in treating Agnes so terribly? Her good intention to be more tolerant of the girl had not succeeded. When her grandfather had told her Agnes might be going to church, her first reaction had been that she didn't want her company. Being so much prettier, even with the cuts and bruises, the older girl might attract Benjamin's attention, now he had taken umbrage with her, although he had not seemed to pay her any attention the day before. But since the incident, he might have changed.

With a sigh, she handed her grandfather his drink. "If Agnes is coming, she'd better make haste. I need to be going now."

The girl in question came downstairs carrying Tommy, both in their Sunday best, although her dress looked familiar.

"Are you taking Tommy?" Harriet asked. "It would delay us, trying to push the perambulator through the snow."

"I 'adn't thought o' that. What a dolt I am." Agnes bit her lip and turned to Gampy. "Are you going, Mister Bond? I don't s'pose...?"

"Give him here." Gampy held out his arms. "I'll look after the little cockalorum. He's no bother."

"Come on, then," urged Harriet, eager to be off.

Agnes checked her hair in the mirror. "But we got plenty of time, ain't we?"

"I want to make sure I'm not late. It takes much longer in the snow."

182

"Does this bonnet suit me?"

"Yes, come on." Another of her mother's things. She'd have nothing to wear when she finally come out of her laying-in period.

"But I ain't sure about the colour."

"Beggars can't be choosers, lass," said Gampy, mirroring the very words Harriet had thought of, but had bitten her tongue to make sure she didn't.

"I 'ain't had no breakfast," continued the girl, still preening herself.

"Look, if you don't come now, I'll go without you," said Harriet, opening the door. "I won't be able to rush, because of my bad ankle, and I don't want to be late, so make up your mind."

Agnes looked from Harriet to Gampy. "What d'yer think, Mister Bond?"

"Don't bring me into it." He shook his head and tucked one of Tommy's curls under his hat. "You girls need to sort it out between you."

Harriet stood in the doorway, hoping the other girl had changed her mind. "Well?"

Agnes blew out her cheeks and grabbed her coat. "S'pose, nah I'm all dressed up, may as well. Lead on. I don't know where the church is, so I can't foller on later."

Eager to make haste, Harriet pulled her coat and shawl tighter to warm her neck. Agnes moaned and chuntered as she slipped and slid in the soft, slushy snow, eventually linking arms for support.

Appreciating the warmth from the other girl, Harriet asked, "Have you been to church before? I was surprised when Gampy said you were coming, 'cos you're not a Catholic, are you?"

"Nah, but me ma used to be, when she were a child."

"You can't say someone 'used to be' a Catholic. Once you've been baptised you remain one for the rest of your life."

"Well, yer know what I means. I ain't even been christened, I don't think."

Afraid she might be contaminated, Harriet pulled away, trying to think of the implications of that statement. "But… are you sure?"

"No, not for certain."

Why did she have to tell her that? Was she even allowed to enter the church? Harriet decided to give her the benefit of the doubt. If she wasn't sure, there was the possibility she might have been, so she clung onto that idea as they continued along the white, almost deserted streets.

Approaching the church, she could see no sign of Benjamin or his mother or father at first. Then they appeared. Would he speak, or ignore her? She stepped forward and nodded to his mother. The lady nodded back. Now him. Joy of joys, he smiled and held out his hand.

"Good day, Miss Harding, Missus…" He turned to Agnes, who smiled sweetly at him, damn the girl, although she hung back behind Harriet. Of course, he didn't know her name, for they hadn't been introduced the day before. Blowed if she was going to do so now, she turned to go inside after repeating his salutation.

A candle lit for her father, and one for her brother, she said a special prayer for them.

If she sat near the back she could sneak out if Agnes made a fool of herself, gave the wrong responses or… She slapped her hand to her mouth. *Oh, heck, I haven't told her she can't receive Holy Communion because she's not a Catholic.* She pulled her into a space at the back of the church and whispered into her ear.

"I'll just follow you," Agnes whispered back.

"No, that's just it, you can't. You'll have to stay in your seat until I return. I'll nudge you. Don't do anything wrong, I beg of you." Especially if he's watching. She moved to sit behind a pillar, as far away from him as possible, to make sure he couldn't see them.

When the priest blessed the incense, she could see Agnes screwing up her face at the smell and hoped she wouldn't say anything. The other girl, however, behaved correctly, much to Harriet's relief. As a little girl, Harriet had asked her mama what the priest was doing and, when her mother whispered in her ear, she thought she said he was blessing the *insects*. Although she hadn't seen any insects on the flowers, it seemed a splendid idea.

Agnes even sang some of the hymns, which amazed her. Perhaps the girl wasn't uncouth after all.

However, when she returned from Holy Communion, the girl had disappeared. In an effort to respect the sacrament, and say her prayers of thanksgiving, she knelt down, but couldn't concentrate. This was the time she looked forward to all week so, as soon as the final hymn had been sung, with gritted teeth, she hurried out, to see Benjamin Toghill talking to...only the very person she wouldn't have wanted him to speak to.

Trying to catch his eye, she waved. When he didn't respond, she ran across. "Ah, there you are, Agnes."

"I hope I didn't worry yer," the girl replied. "I needed a bitta fresh air. Mister Toghill's been entertaining me."

Harriet stood between them, pretending a large lady needed more space to pass. "Has he? What with?" Trying to guess his mood, she looked at him. Those eyes! They were twinkling at her. He must have forgiven her. Surely, he wouldn't twinkle, if not?

"Just a funny story," he replied, as his mother came over.

"Benjamin, I'm going." She studied Harriet's face. "You work in the haberdashery shop, don't you?"

"Yes, Missus Toghill. I hope you found our service satisfactory."

"Certainly. I have been telling all my friends what a lovely establishment it is."

"Thank you, ma'am. Miss Louisa...I mean, Missus Little will be very pleased to hear that." |

Benjamin turned to her. "How is your ankle, Miss Harding? I trust it is recovered?"

"Certainly." Oh, dear, she had repeated what his mother had said. Would she notice?

As the lady in question walked away with a, "Good day to you," she couldn't tell.

"But the walk here has exasperated it, I fear."

With a grin, he corrected her. "I think you mean 'exacerbated'."

"That's what she said, ain't it?" intervened Agnes, clearly not wanting to be left out of the conversation.

"Not quite." He held out his arms. "Would you like me to accompany you ladies to your home?"

Not in her wildest dreams had she imagined him saying that. Well, in the very wildest of them, maybe.

Her heart beating harder than a drum, she replied, "If you're sure, sir. We would not want to put you out."

"It will be my pleasure. I rarely have occasion to escort two such beautiful ladies."

It was not just her he wanted to be with then. She might have known. Agnes gave a little simper behind his back as she grabbed his other arm. They passed his mother, talking to another lady, and he called to tell her his intentions, and they set off. Should she exaggerate a limp? But that would be deceitful. She had just been to Mass and had her soul cleansed.

The weather seemed a solid topic. "I hope this snow goes soon, don't you, sir? Some of us have to make it to work in the morning." Would he take the hint that Agnes had no such worries? "Where do you work?"

"Dear girl, I work in the office of life."

"Really, where's that?"

He laughed. "Actually, I work in my father's law business."

186

"You're a lawyer?"

"Not yet, but I plan to be some day."

No wonder he seemed wealthy. She had heard lawyers were paid top salaries.

"I had an uncle who were a solicitor," Agnes added.

"That's not quite the same," he replied, sending a frisson of pleasure down Harriet's back at the correction.

"'Course not," Harriet said, as if she had known all along.

"I never thought it were," retorted Agnes. "I were just saying."

Benjamin stopped. "Ladies, please, no squabbles on such a fine day. Look at the beautiful blue sky, and listen to the birds singing sweetly in the trees."

Harriet looked around, trying to find a tree, let alone hear a bird.

"See, that's stopped you in your tracks, has it not?" He linked arms once more. "There was a blackbird in the tree near the church. Did you not hear it singing? It is one of the most evocative sounds I know."

"Mister Toghill," replied Harriet, "you must be a poet, to say such delightful things."

"I have my moments. Do you write poetry?"

"Only in school. I never feel inclined at home."

"You should. If ever I marry, I should expect my wife to be conversant with literature in all its forms."

Her face fell and she slowed down, seeing no point in continuing her dream. What had she been thinking of, to even have an inkling that he would entertain her company?

As they turned the corner into Hare Street, she stopped. "Thank you, kind sir, for escorting us home." She fumbled in her purse. "Here's the sixpence I owe you. Thank you very much for lending it to me. We won't keep you any longer. Good day."

He doffed his cap, saying, "It was my pleasure, ma'am. Good day to you both, and my compliments to your mother." For a second, she thought he was about to say something further, but he walked on around the corner, leaving her heart in tatters.

"That were a bit hasty, weren't it?" asked Agnes as they walked towards their house. "You like him, don't yer?"

"I thought I did, but what's the point? He's way out of my reach. You heard him. Any wife of his would have to know about literature. I don't know the heck of a thing about it. I can't write poetry. Goodbye, Mister Benjamin Toghill. It was nice knowing you." With a lump in her throat, she opened the front door.

Lucy called, "Are you coming over later, Harriet? Mama's finished those bootees."

"That's great news. Yes, I will, thank you."

They were greeted by her mother, holding one of the twins. "Hello, dearie, did you have a good service?" Before she could reply, she added, "And how did you enjoy it, Agnes? I didn't know you were a church-goer."

"It were good, fanks, Missus, 'specially wearing your beautiful cloves. I must give 'em back. Can Tommy stay there while I change?"

Tommy sat on the floor playing with a toy train. Harriet recognised it as belonging to her baby brother who had died, also a Tommy. "I need to change as well. I'm going across to Lucy's later, unless you need me for anything?"

"You could check on Winifred, while you're upstairs. She was sleeping when I came down."

Halfway up the stairs, she turned to ask, "Is Gampy out?"

"Yes, he popped down to the Princess for some ale."

"Is there anything wrong with him? He doesn't seem well to me."

"He's fine. Don't worry about him."

If her mother thought him to be well, then why was she concerned? An hour with his mates would cheer him up, as long as he didn't roll home in his cups, like he had once. It

188

had been funny to see him, singing one of his sea shanties, unable to stand still, and talking a load of drivel. Not that she knew what he was talking about half the time, anyway, with his made-up cockney rhyming slang.

Checking Winnie, she changed into her everyday dress.

Agnes had also changed and was peeling potatoes. About to make some retort about it being nice to see the girl doing something useful for a change, she held her tongue. "Do you want any help?" she asked, instead.

Agnes pointed to the carrots. "You can peel them."

Harriet picked up a knife. "Carrots again. That's all we ever have. Runner beans or cabbage would make a change."

"Wrong season, in't it."

"Carrots don't grow in winter."

"I don't know, then."

"Me, neither."

They worked amicably until the vegetables had been prepared.

Harriet wiped her hands down her apron and took baby William from her mother. "My, he's growing," she retorted. "He'll soon be as big as Tommy at this rate."

"I'm pleased with his progress. He's such a good baby. I'm so lucky." Her mother's eyes filled with tears. "If only your father were here to see him. He'd be proud of him, and Winnie, of course." Tears fell down her cheeks, and Harriet put her arm around her.

"I miss him too, Mama, and it'll be even worse at Christmas. And our William, of course, although at least we have this William to take his place."

"He could never do that, child. One son can't replace another. You'll learn when you have children of your own."

"That'll never happen."

Not with Benjamin Toghill, anyway.

"What about that young man who called yesterday?"

"He's out of my league, Mama, much too high-brow. I'll never match up to his high standards."

"Someone will come along. You're young yet, only just into womanhood. Are you still having tummy aches?"

"No, they've stopped. I'd almost forgotten about them. Do they happen every time the fairies come?" The baby started to cry, so she tickled him under his chin.

"More than likely, I'm afraid to say." Her mother took the baby. "Just another pitfall of growing into adulthood. It looks as if this one hasn't had enough to eat. At this rate, I might have to call in a wet nurse. It's a good job Tommy takes solids now."

Agnes came through and picked up her son. "I'd like ter visit me ma this afternoon, if I can find 'er, if she ain't in the boozer."

"Good idea," replied Harriet, standing to allow her now-tear-free mother more room to feed the baby. "Maybe she'll ask you to go back. Would you like to?" It had not occurred to her to wonder how the girl felt.

"Yer've all been so good ter me, but I do 'anker after her at times."

"That's only to be understood, dearie," replied her mother. "You only have one mother. Never forget that. She gave birth to you, and you should never fall out with her, no matter how much you resent her attitude. I agree with Harriet. It would be a great idea. Not that you're a nuisance, but I'm sure she would grow to love Tommy, just as we have."

Agnes surprised them both by leaning forward and planting a kiss on her cheek. "Fanks, Missus. I'll make a special effort to be nice to 'er, no matter what she says. Like you says, she's the only ma I got, though you comes near to being one. You're a lovely lady."

Harriet wondered if she were to be included in the praise, but was not shocked when Agnes went into the kitchen without speaking to her. After all, she had treated her abominably, and why? If she searched her conscience, she knew it was due to jealousy, nothing more, nothing less.

190

She had accused Benjamin Toghill of being unchristian, but she had acted even more meanly, and for no reason. Should she apologise? The wretched girl had obviously had a hard time, thrown out by her boozy mother. Who was she to judge? Could she have coped any better in the same circumstances? But she wouldn't have ever found herself so. She would never get pregnant, no matter how much a man persuaded her to do whatever they did to have a baby, not until she was married.

An apology would not come amiss, so she ventured towards her, asking as she reached out, "May I help?"

"What?" Agnes swivelled around, and Harriet could see tears on her cheeks.

"Would you like me to go with you?" A look of amazement shot across the girl's face. She had clearly not expected that. "I'm sorry I've acted in such a childish way," Harriet continued. "I'd like to help you. Not to be rid of you, but to see you settled. What with my pa and brother dying like that, I must have been unbalanced. I'm usually a tolerant person, but I've not treated you as I should. Can you forgive me?"

Agnes wiped her hands across her face and sniffed. "I shouldn't 'ave dumped me problems on yer. I didn't know you was on your own when I first come. I ain't surprised yer don't like me."

"It isn't that I don't like you. I think we could be friends. I'd like us to be."

"I'd like that, too."

Harriet debated if she should hug her, but thought that would be going too far, too soon, so she patted her arm and checked whether the dinner needed attention.

"Will Gampy be back for dinner, Mama" she called. "Or shall we leave his to keep warm over a pan of water?"

"I hope so. We'll hang on for a while, just in case."

Baby William had fallen asleep, and her mother looked as though she could as well. Harriet took the baby and cuddled him.

Her mother stood up. "On second thoughts, I'll go back to bed for a while before Winnie wakes up. I'll have my dinner later."

"Are you sure, Mama? You should eat something. How about a cracker or a biscuit"

"Very well, just to keep me going."

Harriet found a few fragments of soft gingerbread, all that remained in the bottom of the tin. "Maybe I should have bought biscuits instead of stupid porridge yesterday," she muttered as she handed it to her mother, waiting on the stairs.

Gampy had still not returned by the time dinner was ready, so Harriet and Agnes sat down together. How good it felt to be friends instead of resenting her. They chatted about Agnes's brothers and sisters and her mother's new man.

"It must be nice to have sisters," remarked Harriet as she chewed on a piece of hard carrot that hadn't cooked properly. "I only had William up to now, before Winifred came along, but she's only little, of course. All the others died as babies."

"Mine are all little, too. I've really enjoyed livin' 'ere. I knows you weren't very happy about me comin', but I 'opes you've changed yer mind a bit."

"You're sort of my sister now, or would have been if you'd married William, so we'll put the past behind us." Harriet smiled and patted the girl's hand. "I can't imagine what it was like living rough. We don't have much money, though more than others, so I count myself fortunate."

Agnes related some of the events she had witnessed whilst huddling in doorways, such as fights amongst the other homeless, men and women. "Sometimes women was worse than the men," she said, sitting back and shaking her head. "I don't want to do that again."

"If your ma won't take you back, you can always return here. Gampy's taken a shine to you. That's why I was jealous. I've always been his little girl."

"Yer lucky, 'avin' such a wonderful fam'ly."

"Yes, I am, and I never appreciated it before you came. You'd have loved Papa, God rest his soul. He could be strict at times, especially over manners, like don't talk with your mouthful of food, and don't use both hands to eat a sandwich. 'You are not a dog with a bone,' he would say.' But he always loved me, no matter what." She took a deep breath, fighting against tears. "I hope Gampy's having a good time, because his dinner's cold. I'd better put it to warm." She took his plate to the range and put it, with her mother's, over pans of hot water, wondering whether to ask Agnes if she thought he seemed well. But she wouldn't know what he used to be like, so would have nothing with which to compare his present state.

Two hours later, he reeled in, singing. "'What shall we do with a drunken sailor? What shall we do with a drunken sailor? What shall we do with a drunken sailor? Early in the morning'. Hello, girlie, how's you doing?"

"Gampy, you're drunk," she admonished him, hands on hips. "I suppose you don't want your dried-up dinner."

"Dinner, winner, sinner, call it what you like." He slumped into the armchair. "I don't want nothing. I ain't got the stomach for it. Where's your ma?"

"She's upstairs, and Agnes has gone out with Tommy. Both the babies are asleep and I was sitting here on my dog and bone, trying to knit this jacket for baby Winnie. I hoped you might help. You're good with your hands, but in your condition there'd be twice as many dropped stitches."

"Don't try to use lemon and lime, girlie; it don't sound right on you."

She sat down, shaking her head in disgust. He didn't usually drink to such an extent. But maybe it would cure whatever seemed to be ailing him. Snores soon erupted from the chair, and she covered him with one of Tommy's blankets, after giving his beard a stroke. "You deserve a binge now and again, what with having to put up with all of us," she whispered.

Gampy safely tucked up, she put on her coat. How much money would Missus Bowe want for making the bootees? Should she take any? No, better to come back for it, if she did want paying. She opened the front door as quietly as she could, although, given the state of her grandfather, he wouldn't hear an earthquake.

"Come in, come in," greeted Missus Bowe as Harriet clanked her door knocker. "What's the weather doing?"

"It isn't snowing but what's there is too stubborn to go away."

"Ah, well, I suppose it's better than fog. That makes me cough. I hate it."

"Yes, it isn't healthy."

"How's your ma and the babies?"

Harriet could see Lucy gesticulating to her behind her mother's back. Trying to keep from grinning, she replied, "Mama's well, but tired, thank you, and the twins are thriving, although Winifred isn't as robust as William."

Lucy pulled her away and dragged her through the smoky room, past her snoring father, through to the kitchen. "I've something to tell you," she hissed as she closed the dividing door. "You'll never guess."

Harriet racked her brain. "Um…you've won that thingy they used to do, where they won lots of money? What was it called? The lottery?"

"No, silly, but I wish they still ran it. My great grandfather used to often win. In fact, Ma told me he… But never mind that. Guess what's happened?"

"You're walking out with that boy you fancied?"

194

Lucy's mouth drooped. "Well, no, but he smiled at me."

Harriet grinned. "Is that all? I used to be besotted with a boy. I think I told you about him, the one from church with the gorgeous blue eyes?"

"Yes, but you're too young to know what it feels like."

"Well, I've advanced further than you, if all you've had is a smile."

Lucy gave her an incredulous glare, and pulled her down to sit at the table. "Really? Tell me more."

Harriet related the events of the day before.

"He's the one I saw you with, walking brazenly down the street, unaccompanied. And did you see him this morning at church?"

Harriet stuck out her bottom lip and sighed. "Yes, but it all ended disastrously. He wants a wife who is 'conversant with literature in all its forms'. I remember his words exactly."

Lucy pulled at her upper lip, as realisation dawned on her. "And you can't read, let alone spout poetry or anything."

"Of course I can read. I'm not a complete duffer."

"Well, get off to the library then. Borrow as many books as you can."

"I hadn't thought of that. But which ones? I mean, there's thousands."

Lucy turned from filling the kettle. "Did he give any indication as to his preferences?"

"Ooer, Lucy, who's coming over all illiterate?"

"I think you mean 'literate', my dear."

"You see. I can't even talk proper. What chance do I have? Anyway, we were talking about poetry. The only poems I've read were the ones we learnt in school. Can you remember any?"

"I loved that one about the daffodils. Wordsworth, I think." Lucy sipped her tea and stared dreamily out of the window. "How I'd love to live near mountains and lakes, and watch flowers 'fluttering and dancing in the breeze', wouldn't you?"

"Mm, instead of the foggy, black filth of London. That was one of my favourites, although I liked the one about the Ancient Mariner because it reminded me of Gampy, him being a sailor and all."

"See, you do know about poetry."

"But how can I go to the library, when I'm at work all day?"

"Ask if you can go at lunch time. That's what I do, if I need anything."

Harriet hugged her friend. "Lucy, you're a marvel. Why ever I didn't think of that, I don't know. I'll start tomorrow. His name's Benjamin Toghill, by the way. Just fancy..." it was her turn to look dreamily out of the window "...Missus Harriet Toghill. Doesn't that sound perfect?"

"It does have a certain ring to it. Now we've sorted out your problem, what can we do about mine?"

Missus Bowe interrupted them. "I see you've already partaked. Where's my cuppa, then?"

Lucy jumped up, crying, "Sorry, Ma," as she poured out another drink. "Will Pa want one?"

"Nah, he's still asleep. Leave him while we can." A certain look went from mother to daughter.

Harriet knew exactly what it meant. They didn't want his bad mood to spoil their Sunday afternoon.

"Did Lucy tell you I've finished the bootees?"

"Yes, thank you, Missus Bowe. How much do I owe you?"

The lady waved her hand in dismissal. "Nothing, my dear. I used wool from an old jumper I unpicked. I hope the colour suits. It's a sort of yellow. They're in there," she pointed towards the front room. "I'll fetch them when his lordship awakes." She took down a red biscuit tin from the shelf and opened it.

The smell of spices filled the kitchen. "Oo, thank you. I love your spicy biscuits. I've tried making them, but they never seem as nice as yours."

"It's my grandmother's special recipe. I've never tasted anything like them anywhere."

They sat munching away, lost in their own thoughts for a while, until Lucy suggested a walk.

"Yes, catch some fresh air, while the sun's shining," answered her mother. "You can't beat a bout of fresh air to ward off bad humours. I'll come with you."

Lucy grimaced at Harriet, but said nothing. Their chat would have to wait. Harriet wondered when her friend could have seen the young man in question. It must have been the previous day, when she'd been on cloud nine herself, walking out with Benjamin Toghill. Well, not walking out, but walking with, the subtle difference not lost on her.

Chapter 22

An intangible sound woke Harriet. Unable to identify it, she sat up in bed. Her mother was sleeping peacefully, and little snorts and grunts came from the twins in their cradle at the bottom of the bed, so it couldn't have been them. She pushed aside the blankets and, pulling her nightgown around her, crept onto the landing. All quiet. Maybe she'd been dreaming. She tiptoed back into the bedroom. But something made her turn back, and she grabbed the dressing gown from the back of the door and crept downstairs, not wanting to wake her grandfather.

As her eyes adjusted to the darkness, she could make him out, fast asleep, although one of his arms hung outside his covers. It felt icy cold, and when she tried to move it, it was stiff. "You poor man," she whispered. "You're so cold your arm's frozen solid." She prodded the fire with the poker, but it had gone out, not a spark of red. As she wondered whether to relight it, a terrible thought occurred to her and, turning back, she ran her fingers down her grandfather's face and neck, inside his nightshirt to his chest. Cold as ice. A chill ran through her and she dropped onto the floor beside him. "No, Gampy, no. Please don't be dead. You can't die. We need you."

Dropping to her knees, she prayed for his soul to reach Heaven straightaway, and wrapped the edge of his blanket around her, awakening later with pins and needles in her leg from the cramped position. He wouldn't need the blanket any more, but feeling his face to make sure, she wrapped herself up in it and sat in the armchair, prepared to sit out the night in vigil.

The clock told her she should be rising to prepare herself for work. But she couldn't leave Gampy. Agnes had brought Tommy back, not having been reconciled with her mother. He stirred, but she didn't have time to see to him; she needed to tell Mama her father had passed away, or whatever appropriate expression she could think of. Which would be the least upsetting? Gone to Heaven—that seemed a good way of saying it. Better than some of the others, like 'kicked the bucket' or such irreverent sayings.

About to draw back the curtains, she stopped. They would have to be closed all day, at least until Gampy had been laid out. Mirrors should be covered, as well, but she didn't believe his spirit would be trapped in the reflective glass. His soul would already be in Heaven, or at least, on its way, maybe waiting in Purgatory until he had atoned for his sins.

She approached the stairs and slowly crept up, her heart beating fast as she prepared to give her mother the bad news. Blood could be tasted on her lip. She must have bitten it in her anguish. How could she turn her world upside down again, so soon after William Henry and Papa?

Her mother sat in her feeding chair with one of the twins. "Hello," she smiled. Seeing Harriet's face, her brow furrowed. "What on earth is the matter? You're as white as a sheet."

"It's Gampy, Mama. I don't know how to tell you, but he's..." Tears fell down her cheeks as she let out her breath. "I wish it could be otherwise, but I'm afraid he's died."

"Died? My father, my wonderful, loving father? Are you sure? How do you know?"

"Because..." She knelt down and stroked her hand. "Because I've been with him all night, since I had a feeling, a sort of premonition, and I went down and found him stone cold. Should I fetch Old Mother Peele? Or do you want to check first?"

Her mother stared into space, as if she had not heard. Harriet couldn't believe her ears when she did reply, "What were you thinking of, child, to be spending the night with him in his state?"

Criticism? That wasn't what she wanted. She needed reassurance that she had done the right thing. "But, Mama, I didn't think I should wake you, and why shouldn't I stay with him. I love him. I didn't want him to be alone all night, even though Tommy was there, but he was asleep."

"Thank goodness for that."

Harriet couldn't understand her mother's attitude. She'd expected her to wail and cry, not show the cold, seemingly unemotional face she could see before her. "Shall I fetch Old Mother Peele or not?"

Her mother nodded as Agnes popped her head around the door and asked, "Is everything alright?"

With a shake of her head, Harriet replied, "No, but Mama doesn't seem able to take in the news. Gampy's dead."

"Dead? What d'yer mean? He were well last night when I come to bed."

"Well, he isn't now. Please stay with Mama while I fetch Old Mother Peele."

"What about Tommy? Is he still downstairs with…?"

"Yes, you'd better bring him up."

She pulled on a dress and Agnes quickly fastened the buttons. Not bothering with a coat, she ran across the street to the old sage's house and rapped on the door.

It opened straightaway. "I s'pose you're in need of my services," declared the old lady.

"How do you know?" she asked in amazement.

"Ah, that'd be telling." She touched the side of her nose. "Is it the baby girl?"

"No." *Got you. You're not as clever as you thought.* "It's my grandfather."

"Well, I knew it would be one or the other. How long?"

"Since the middle of the night. I don't know exactly what time."

They dodged the build up of traffic speeding along the street, oblivious to her sorrow and pain. A funeral coach went past, empty, but with enough foreboding to catch her breath.

They entered the house, still shrouded in darkness, with just the candle lit.

"How's your mother taken it?" asked Old Mother Peele.

"Well, she seemed in a state of shock when I told her, especially when I said I'd stayed with him all night. But I couldn't leave him on his own, could I? What do you say?"

"I says you do as you thinks fit. If it comforts you, then that's the right action to take."

"Thank you." Harriet watched as the old lady examined her grandfather, then asked, "Would you like a cup of tea? I'm going to make a pot."

"No, ta," she replied. "Have you called a doctor to certify the death?"

"No, I thought you'd do that."

"I ain't a doctor. You need him first, before I can do anything. Nip out now, while I fetch my stuff. He is most certainly dead, though. I can tell you that."

Harriet ran to the doctor's house and found him locking his door. He agreed to accompany her and certified that Gampy had died from old age.

After he had gone, Harriet stroked her grandfather's arm. He looked as if he were smiling, even through the beard, and must have died peacefully, probably dreaming about the ocean waves he loved so much. He would have no more stories to tell her. She would have to remember them all. Maybe she'd be allowed to tell one or two at his funeral, if she was allowed to go. That would please her. She thought back the short space of time since the last one—her father's. Why did people she loved have to die? Was God punishing her? For imagining herself to be the Virgin Mary? Had she committed a mortal sin in doing so? Or in being so horrid to Agnes?

201

Her thoughts were interrupted by the front door opening. She stood up to allow Old Mother Peele to perform her duties and went through to the kitchen. Her mother would be in dire need of a drink, so she must not delay.

She squeezed past the old lady and took the tray upstairs.

"What shall I do about work?" she asked her mother who sat cradling Winnie. "Should I go?"

"I suppose so."

"So, it's all right, then? Carry on as if nothing's happened?"

"Did I say that?"

"No, Mama, I'm sorry. I just…" Harriet broke down, sobbing, as her mother lay Winnie on the bed and enfolded her in her arms.

Never again would she sit on her grandfather's knee, holding a long stick with a piece of string tied to it, fishing in dry water in the wicker wastepaper basket, while he sang a ditty about a dark-haired girl with her hair in a curl, who worked a sewing machine. Nor would she listen to his yarns, imagining herself whisked away to those far-off lands where people wore turbans, and spoke with an unusual accent; or smell the aroma of spices as he described the noisy markets and the hustle and bustle of hot bodies all vying for trade. Once he'd said he would bring her back a monkey, but that had never happened. How she would have petted it, as if it were a baby.

She sat up and wiped her eyes on her sleeve. Two, no, three babies, needed her more than a monkey would have. She had to remain strong for them, for her mother, and even for Agnes. "What do I do about arranging the funeral, Mama?"

"Nothing, dearie. I'll pull myself together and sort it out. I've languished up here for too long. It's time I…" Tears flowed down her mother's face once more. However strong she hoped she'd be, Harriet knew it would be some time before she'd be her old self. Having the twins had taken it out of her.

"Are you sure, Mama? It's only been a few weeks since the twins were born, are you sure you feel up to it? I'm sure Old Mother Peele will help."

"No, no, he was my father. I'll manage, but I don't know how we'll pay for it."

"Gampy said he had money, but where would he have kept it?"

"Maybe we should have questioned him. I know one thing: he didn't have anything to do with them banks. Pop down and ask Old Mother Peele to check in his pockets before she finishes laying him out. I should hate to bury it with him."

Harriet dashed downstairs. The old sage hummed as she performed her task, as if she enjoyed it. Ugh. Harriet couldn't think of a worse job, other than the nightsoil men's, or the sewer workers she'd seen. She dared not disturb her, and how could she broach the subject without appearing tactless or greedy?

With Tommy crying, cradled in her arms, Agnes came downstairs as she stood dithering. "'E's 'ungry. Sorry ter interrupt, but I need to find 'im a bite to eat." Her face a picture of horror, she sidled past Old Mother Peele who ignored her, wiping the white body in seemingly disrespectful haste. Harriet thought she should be doing it tenderly. But the old lady had not loved him as she had, so it was only a job to her.

As soon as she straightened, Harriet dived in. "Old Mother Peele, did you check the pockets?"

The old sage delved into her apron and grinned, showing a row of broken teeth, with large gaps. "You mean, did he have any money on him?"

With bated breath, she nodded, her shoulders drooping with disgust at being concerned with such a topic when her dear old grandfather lay there, dead.

"Apart from a few pennies, this is all I found." The old lady held out a tatty, brown folded envelope. "I can't see his fortune being in there."

Hardly daring to examine it, Harriet took it between her finger and thumb. "I'll take it to Mama, and let her check inside."

"As long as there's enough money for my fee, I ain't bothered. I'll have that cuppa now, if I may."

Harriet called for Agnes to pour one and went upstairs, to be met by her mother.

"What did she say?" her mother whispered as she handed over the package. "Let's go back in here and open it."

"Old Mother Peele says she wants paying first. How much will that cost?" Harriet whispered back as her mother shrugged, gingerly unfolded the envelope, and opened it. Three pound notes fell out and a note. "Three pounds won't keep us going for long. What does the note say?" She sat on the bed beside her mother and tried to read the scrawly writing.

"Not a lot, from what I can make out." Her mother pointed to a particularly illegible scrawl. "What's that word?"

"Um, I don't know. Should we ask Old Mother Whatsit?"

Her mother cupped her chin and pursed her lips. "Do we really want her knowing all our business?"

"But, Mama, we won't know if we can't work out what it says. And there's no point asking Agnes. She can't read at all."

"True, very true." They had another go at the words, but to no avail, so they took it downstairs, where they found Agnes and the old lady in the kitchen. "Um, Mistress

Peele," began her mother, surprising Harriet, for she had only ever known the lady as Old Mother, "would you do me a favour, and decipher this note, for neither I nor Harriet can make head nor tail of it?"

She handed over the piece of grubby paper and the old lady studied it, squinting. "Not without me specs, I can't. Sorry."

Agnes made as if to take it, but Harriet snatched it back, hissing, in a sharper voice than she had intended, "You can't read or write, so there's no point in you looking at it."

Missus Edwards from next door peeped through the kitchen window. "I think she can read," remarked Harriet. "Shall we ask her?"

"Yes, why not let the whole street know our affairs?"

"Mama, please don't be upset."

Missus Edwards from next door came inside but stopped with a look of confusion on her face upon seeing Old Mother Peele. "Oh, I didn't realise... Pray excuse me. Is all well? I mean...?"

"It's my father, God rest his soul," muttered her mother, blessing herself with the sign of the cross.

The neighbour's face dropped. "I'm sorry to hear that. Would you like me to take young Tommy out of your way for a while? I'm sure you have stuff to do and people to see, and I'd be only too glad to mind him for a while."

They all turned to look at Agnes who replied, "Fanks, Missus." She stood up and the neighbour held out her arms to take the baby, but Agnes continued, "I'll come wiv yer. I'm in the way 'ere. There's nofink I can do, and I ain't comftable with dead bodies lyin' abaht."

"Nor are any of us," replied Harriet. "But, before you go, Missus Edwards, please could you take a look at this note? We can't work out what it says, and wondered if you'd be able to."

The lady took the paper. "I think it's…it looks like the name of a solicitor, Id say. Yes, Somerfield and Pl…Plankett, or something like that, on Brick Lane."

"A solicitor?" squealed her mother. "Why would he have a solicitor's name on a piece of paper?"

Old Mother Peele stood up. "Maybe he left a will, leaving you thousands of pounds."

"He once said something about a will. I didn't know what he was talking about, and he didn't enlarge on it, and it was never spoken about again. Do you really think that could be it?" Her mother squeezed her hands together. "But we shouldn't be thinking of that, not while he's lying there. I'd better pop to the carpenter up the street. We'll need a coffin."

Agnes and the neighbour left but Old Mother Peele hovered, probably waiting for her money. Harriet looked at her mother, who delved behind the crockery on the sideboard, found a tin, and took out a handful of copper coins. She held them out to the lady and allowed her to take what she wanted.

"I only wants me expenses, you know, for me oils and the shroud and stuff."

Her mother sighed as she looked at the few coins left in her hand. "I know. I wouldn't expect you to do it for nothing."

Chapter 23

On her way home from Midnight Mass, Harriet hurried along the dark streets with Agnes at her side. At half past one in the morning on Christmas Day they were mostly deserted. Only a few vagrants and one or two revellers, the worse for drink, frequented them at that time of the night.

"We should have brought a lantern," she remarked, after almost tripping.

"You said the light from the moon'd be enough," replied Agnes, looking up at the black sky. "But there don't seem to be one tonight."

"No, there don't...I mean, doesn't, more's the pity. At least that awful fog that's been covering us for the last few days has gone. That was a right pea-souper."

"Harriet?" Agnes asked with a query in her voice.

"That's my name, don't wear it out."

"Pardon?"

"Nothing. I heard someone use that expression once, and I've always wanted to say it." They crossed the road and hastened even faster, the cold wind cutting through their new clothes.

The names on the note they had found in Gampy's pocket had indeed been a firm of solicitors on Brick Lane. They had been amazed when his will had been read out, to find he had left a substantial amount of money to her mother, who had promptly taken them on a trip to the dress shop to buy a new dress each. Harriet would still need to work, otherwise the windfall would soon run out. Agnes had been successful in obtaining a job and had started a few days before, working in the mill. It would mean her mama would have to look after all three babies, but Missus Edwards from next door had offered to take Tommy as much as possible.

As they rounded the corner of Hare Street, she asked what Agnes had been about to say.

"It were just what the priest said. Did I hear right? The mother of Jesus were a virgin?"

"Yes, whatever that means. Her name was Mary."

"'Ow could that 'appen?"

Harriet shrugged as they entered the quiet house. Her mother had intended to wait up for them, but she must have been too tired. She lit a candle. "It's just one of those stories you believe, a sort of miracle." She picked up one of the presents under the Christmas tree. "When I was a little girl, I was allowed to open a present when we came back from Midnight Mass. Shall we open one?"

Agnes hung her head. "I don't deserve none."

"Maybe we should wait until Mama and the babies are all together. I'm off to bed, then. Are you looking forward to your brothers and sisters coming this afternoon?"

Agnes smiled as she went towards the stairs. "Yeh, it were thoughtful of yer ma to invite 'em. They're comin' 'bout two o'clock." She picked up her sleeping baby. "I'll let 'im sleep with me, tonight, as a Christmas treat. I can't give 'im much else."

Lying in bed beside her snoring mother, for she still hadn't moved into Agnes's room, Harriet wondered where they would put everybody for dinner. She couldn't remember how many brothers and sisters Agnes had, but most of them were small, and wouldn't take up too much room. Her mother had indeed been generous in inviting them. She herself would not have even considered such an action, which showed how much more thoughtful her mother was.

She dropped to sleep, after saying special prayers for her wonderful grandfather and for her father and brother.

When she awoke, she found her mother already dressing. "Where are you going, Mama?" she asked in astonishment.

"To Mass, of course."

"I hadn't realised you were going. I'll come too. Are we taking the babies?"

"Yes, I need to speak to Father Lane about arranging their baptisms. I should have done it ages ago, especially with Winifred being so poorly, but she's pulled through. The immediate danger has passed."

Harriet pulled on her dress as her mother changed William's clothes. "Agnes seemed to enjoy Midnight Mass," she told her. "Maybe she'll become a convert. Baby Tommy could be christened at the same time."

"Well, he can be christened anyway, even if she doesn't. Pass me that nappy pin, please."

Harriet did as bid and picked up the other baby. "You're going on your first outing, Winnie," she crooned. "And it's to a very special place. I hope you behave, and don't cry and disturb all those people saying their prayers."

Her mother grinned. "I hope they both behave themselves." She reached over and planted a kiss on Harriet's cheek. "Happy Christmas, darling."

"Happy Christmas, Mama." Harriet returned the kiss and gave the babies one as well. "And to you two."

"I know it won't be the same without your father and brother and grandfather, but we must make the best of it."

"Yes." Harriet looked up at the corner, where she had imagined her father's ghost to be, and her mother followed her gaze. She hadn't seen him as well, had she?

"Come on, then, let us go forth," declared her mother. "I'm looking forward to this."

Agnes hadn't come down and, since she had taken Tommy upstairs, they put the twins in his pram, after changing the grubby sheet. William settled down straightaway, but Winifred did not seem to want to sleep. "She's excited, Mama. She must know it's Christmas." Harriet pointed to the holly and ivy with which they had adorned the picture rails and covered the pictures the day before.

"Hurry up, we'll be late," rebuked her mother, pulling on her black coat and bonnet. "Thank goodness all that snow's gone," she added as she opened the door. "Just breathe in that fresh air. I feel as if I've been cooped up here for months."

"Well, you have almost, Mama. Except for Gampy's funeral, you haven't been out."

As they passed the Leekes's house, Isobel came out, followed by her mother. "Happy Christmas," the little girl called.

"Happy Christmas," they returned the greeting.

"Are you off to church?" asked Missus Leekes.

"Yes, and we're late. Farewell."

Their friends turned in the opposite direction. "So are we."

"I didn't know they were church-goers," remarked Harriet. "I wonder which one they attend."

"I don't know, and we haven't time to ponder," replied her mother, pushing the pram even harder.

"Would you like me to push it, Mama?" asked Harriet, worried that her mother would have an apoplexy.

"No, no, dearie. I'm fine."

They arrived at the church in time, and sat near the back, in case one of the babies created a rumpus, but they both slept through.

During the service Harriet spotted Benjamin near the front, and wondered whether to hang around and speak to him.

As she waited with the pram while her mother went to arrange the christenings with the priest, he came across.

"Happy Christmas, Miss Harding."

Her heart beat faster and, feeling her face redden, she kept her head down as she mumbled a reply.

"I trust you are well?" When she nodded, he continued, "I was so sorry to hear about your grandfather's death. My condolences to you and your mother."

Her head shot up. "Thank you. Yes, it's been a very sad time, these past months."

The look of sympathy on his face brought tears to her eyes. He held out his hand and she squeezed it. Her New Year's resolution would definitely be to go to the library, each day, if necessary, to read as many books as she could. Lucy's suggestion had been brilliant, and she had already been into the one near the haberdashery a few days before. When she had suggested it to Miss Louisa, she had given her half an hour's lunch break once a week, encouraging her in her quest. Maybe she could make herself worthy of him. In fact, she would make sure she did.

She wanted to hug him but, of course, could not, so smiled into his gorgeous blue eyes, in a silent plea to ask him to wait for her.

He smiled back and they remained still for a moment, staring at each other in silence.

Her mother rejoined her and, with a wave they set off home.

"You're still friends, then?" asked her mother.

"Oh, yes, Mama. I want to marry him, if he'll have me, when I've read all the books in the library."

Her mother laughed, but did not dispute her statement, giving her even more hope that one day it might happen.

Agnes had tidied up when they returned, and the house was spick and span. Her ma had declined the offer to dine with them, saying she would prefer to stay with her new man, but she had readily agreed to the children coming, probably to give her a few hours of peace. Three babies were taxing, so all those youngsters must take the strength out of a woman.

"I'm popping round to Lucy's, Mama," she said, "while I still have my coat and bonnet on."

Her friend welcomed her inside. "Isn't Christmas exciting?" She twizzled around, showing off a purple dress Harriet hadn't seen before. "Don't you love my new frock?"

"It's beautiful." She felt the fabric. "It's so soft, but not really suitable for winter, is it?"

"Piffle, I don't care."

Harriet could see a small rip under the arm, but she didn't mention it. Her friend's parents could not have afforded such a brand-new item of clothing. They danced around the room, singing and laughing, until Mister Bowe coughed loudly—her cue to leave.

"Did the bootees fit?" asked Missus Bowe, looking up from her knitting. Harriet had heard her singing when she and Lucy had been careering around the room.

"I haven't had time to try them yet, Missus Bowe. We're going to unwrap them later. But I'm sure they will. Thank you very much. I hope you all have a lovely day," she called as she left.

They opened their presents. Agnes had embroidered a handkerchief with a little flower in one corner for Harriet and her mama. Where she had obtained the white linen, Harriet did not like to ask, but the silks had probably come from her mama's sewing box.

Harriet had bought her mother a beautiful black parasol from the second-hand shop along from the haberdashery, and hoped she would not see the little hole at the top. For Tommy, she had bought a brightly-coloured rattle. Agnes had been the biggest problem, and she had finally decided on a pair of red knitted gloves, for the poor girl's hands were always red and chaffed, with more chilblains than she had.

Miss Louisa had given her a present—a pair of soft, kid gloves, that she tried not to show off, in case Agnes considered her knitted ones to be inferior.

The main present she left until last—the one from her mother. What could it be? Quite large, and round. She ripped off the brown paper to reveal a box. On opening it, she gasped. "Mama, it's gorgeous."

"You won't be able to wear it for a while, until your mourning period's over. Do you really like it?"

"Yes, thank you, Mama, I love it. I can't wait to wear it to church to look good for Benjamin." Harriet put on the burgundy hat, trimmed with feathers, and sneaked a peek behind the sheet covering the mirror. Never in her life had she ever envisaged wearing such an item, and she wondered if she might get away with doing so before the end of the six-month period.

Harriet helped Agnes set the table and, after feeding the twins, her mother joined them. More children than she had expected arrived as she dished out dinner. Agnes introduced each one and she tried to memorise their names. They didn't look clean, especially the boys, so she made them all wash their hands and faces in a bowl of water, uncaring if Agnes thought her pernickety.

The goose was cooked to perfection, but she worried there might not be enough to go around. Still, as long as her mother had her fair share, she'd divide the remainder between the rest of them. The children would be unused to much meat, if any at all, so too much would be bad for them.

The little ones sat on the floor. Agnes took the smallest one onto her knee, and Harriet debated whether to do the same with one of the others, but her new dress might have become creased, or worse.

The delight on their faces as they tucked in made the effort of preparing it worthwhile.

They raised their glasses of water and toasted lost loved ones. The children, of course, did not know to whom she referred, but the adults did, and they sat in silence for a few moments, each lost in their own memories.

"What a wonderful hale and hearty, as Gampy would have said," she pronounced. "I'm going to miss his rhymes, so I'd better think up a few of my own."

Chapter 24

5 years later

Benjamin put his arm around Harriet. "Are you happy, my darling?"

"Blissfully." She reached up and kissed him. "It's been rather hectic since we came back from our honeymoon, moving in to this lovely big house and arranging it to our satisfaction. Thank you for being patient."

"You're worth it, my love," he grinned.

Torn between sorrow for Miss Louisa who had died in a horrific road accident, along with her husband, and absolute surprise and delight that her friend had left her the shop in her will, Harriet couldn't believe how her life had turned round.

She tickled his beard. "You don't object to me helping Mama in the shop, do you? I did ask if she wanted to live here with us, but she said she relished her independence. The upstairs space still needs a little work but it's perfect for her and the twins."

"Yes, my love, perfect."

They sat cuddling on the sofa. "I bet you wouldn't have married me if I still lived on Hare Street, would you?" she asked, looking into his gorgeous blue eyes.

"I…"

"Admit it. Your mother would never have allowed it."

"I'm not so sure. She's always known how I feel about you."

"But feelings aren't always taken into account where breeding and status are concerned. Anyway, when are the new cook and the maids arriving?"

"Tomorrow." He kissed her on the neck.

"Erm...Agnes is coming tomorrow, with Toby and the children, but that won't be until Tommy comes home from school. They make such a lovely couple, her and Toby. It's a pity they can't come more often."

Agnes had been introduced to Toby three years before, when her brother had been on leave from the army. Apparently, he had also been a friend of William Henry's.

"If it was left to you, my darling, you'd have the whole of the East End living here."

She laughed and snuggled against him. "Their little Beth's a treasure. Maybe we might have a little one like her in the near future?"

"As long as she has your..." Pushing her away, he looked into her eyes. "But... You're not telling me...?"

She nodded. "I think so. Are you pleased?"

He jumped up and swung her around. "Pleased? I couldn't be happier."

"Even if it's twins?"

"Double the pleasure."

Author Biography

Married to Don, I have 5 children and 9 grandchildren, I live in Derbyshire, England, and enjoy researching my family tree (having found ancestors as far back as 1520), reading, gardening, playing Scrabble, meals out and family gatherings. I am the treasurer of my writing club, Eastwood Writers' Group, and I also write and record Thoughts for the Day for Radio Nottingham. At church I sing in the choir and am an Extraordinary Minister of Holy Communion, a reader, a flower arranger and a member of the fundraising team for Cafod, my favourite charity. I have written hymns, although I cannot read music.

You can see a list of my other books at the front of this one. They are all available on Amazon:

https://www.amazon.co.uk/Angela-Rigley/e/B00607O51M/ref=sr_ntt_srch_lnk_1?qid=1540287989&sr=1-1

Barnes and Noble:

https://www.barnesandnoble.com/s/%22Angela%20Rigley%22?Ntk=P_key_Contributor_List&Ns=P_Sales_Rank&Ntx=mode+matchall

Find me on Twitter: @angierigley; Facebook; LinkedIn. My website is www.nunkynoo.yolasite.com where you can see lots of pictures of lambs and birds, and some of my Thoughts for the Day, and my blog is:

https://wordpress.com/view/authoryantics.wordpress.com

If you enjoyed reading about Harriet – or even if you didn't – I would love it if you could find the time to post a review on Amazon or Goodreads.

Here are some reviews for Nancie, my other YA novel:

Fate deals Nancie many hard blows, and Angela takes us on Nancie's journey through a troubled childhood. Nancie takes it all in her stride, without being overly sentimental. Will life ever get better for her? I couldn't wait to find out. This is my favourite Angela Rigley novel. *Lyn*

A well written and researched book. So well is the period of this book described a wonderful picture comes into your mind of difficult times, dreams and laughter. I do not think a book has made me laugh out loud as this one did. A must read for all lovers of this period and lovers of a gripping story, one that takes your imagination and mind into Victorian England, with beautiful scenery, characters you will not forget plus an ending that leads you to want more. Well done to the author. *Kasia*

https://www.amazon.co.uk/Nancie-Angela-M-Rigley/dp/1511774541/ref=sr_1_5_twi_pap_2?ie=UTF8&qid=1540287066&sr=8-5&keywords=angela+rigley

Printed in Great Britain
by Amazon